the
SCIENCE
of Being
ANGRY

the SCIENCE *of Being* ANGRY

Nicole Melleby

Algonquin Young Readers 2022

Published by
Algonquin Young Readers
an imprint of Algonquin Books of Chapel Hill
Post Office Box 2225
Chapel Hill, North Carolina 27515-2225

a division of
Workman Publishing
225 Varick Street
New York, New York 10014

LIBRARY OF CONGRESS CATALOGING-IN-PUBLICATION DATA

Names: Melleby, Nicole, author.
Title: The science of being angry / Nicole Melleby.
Description: First edition. | Chapel Hill, North Carolina :
Algonquin Young Readers, 2022. | Audience: Ages 9–12. |
Audience: Grades 4–6. | Summary: Eleven-year-old Joey navigates
family, friendships, and her first crush, while looking for answers to
why she feels so angry sometimes and by searching for the donor
her moms chose.
Identifiers: LCCN 2021055851 | ISBN 9781643750378 (hardcover) |
ISBN 9781643752860 (ebook)
Subjects: CYAC: Anger—Fiction. | Family life—Fiction. | Lesbian
mothers—Fiction. | Brothers and sisters—Fiction. | Interpersonal
relations—Fiction. | LCGFT: Fiction.
Classification: LCC PZ7.1.M46934 Sc 2022 | DDC [Fic]—dc23
LC record available at https://lccn.loc.gov/2021055851

10 9 8 7 6 5 4 3 2 1

First Edition

To my family,
the one I was born with
and the one that I made.

the
SCIENCE
of Being
ANGRY

"This is a terrible idea."

Joey ignored her brother. Colton, her other brother, did, too, because they always ignored Thomas in moments like these. Thomas thought everything was a terrible idea. He usually went along with it, anyway, because he hated feeling like the third wheel. He was like Mama in that way.

There was really no avoiding it though, since they were triplets. They should all have been equals, but it was simple math: three of them meant there was always an odd man out.

Joey and Colton had their toes over the edge of the swimming pool. They were always the first two to do everything. The first two born, the first two to start a fight, the first two to climb out of bed in the middle of the unusually sticky, humid fall night to jump into the apartment swimming pool on a dare. They were like their other mom in that way, regardless of the lack of shared DNA.

The boys, Joey's brothers, were skinny and pale in only their underwear. Joey had one of Mom's old hockey shirts on; it came down to her knees. If it were up to her, she'd just be in her underwear, too. But they were already breaking a lot of rules, and her moms could be ridiculously strict about certain gender-related things, like girls wearing shirts outside, even though they were lesbians.

"On the count of three," Joey said, tugging at the neck of her shirt. She was sweating; they all were. That was why they were out here in the first place.

The apartment-complex pool had been closed since after Labor Day, but it hadn't yet been drained. It was too hot to sleep, and Joey had a view of that pool from her bedroom window. She had climbed out of bed and walked quietly on the pads of her feet to her brothers' bedroom. Colton was breathing loudly. He wasn't snoring, but his mouth was open, and it drove

Joey mad that he could sleep through this heat. Her shirt was damp with sweat.

Thomas, from his bed across the room, had noticed her first. "What are you doing?" he had asked, his voice sleepy.

Joey hadn't responded to him then, either. Instead, she climbed up on top of Colton's bed and started kicking at his legs, trying to get him to wake (both out of jealousy that he was asleep and because she knew if anyone else would agree to do this, it would be him).

"Stop," Colton mumbled, his face buried in the pillow. "What are you doing?"

"I can't sleep," Joey said. "It's too hot."

"You're supposed to do like Mama says," Thomas said. "Think about your toes falling asleep, and then your feet, and then your legs, and then—"

"Yeah, yeah, I know, Thomas," Joey interrupted. Mama thought meditation could fix anything. If not that, then the essential oil diffuser she put in Joey's room. Joey usually turned that off once Mama was in her own bed.

The one in Colton and Thomas's room was turned up high. As if the smell of lavender actually did anything.

"I want to go in the pool."

"You want to *what?*" Thomas asked.

Colton blinked sleepily at her. But then he smiled.

Joey wasn't supposed to have a favorite, but in moments like these, it was probably Colton. "Are you coming or what? I'll dare you."

Colton hesitated for only a moment before climbing out of bed. "Yeah, okay. I'm coming."

Joey was impulsive, but Colton was competitive. She could pretty much dare him to do anything.

(Mama was neither of those things. Thomas either. Joey had recently started keeping track.)

So off they went, out of the boys' bedroom, through the hallway and past the kitchen, lucky enough to completely bypass their moms' bedroom on the other side of their apartment and Benny's room down the hall. Thomas didn't want to come, but Joey didn't want him squealing like he had just last week when she and Colton stayed up all night binge-watching a show on Netflix and Mama had asked why they were so tired the next morning. So, to be safe, Joey basically ordered him to come now. She had been barking orders a lot lately.

Anyway, it was kind of good Thomas came, since it was his idea to take their clothes off.

"Mom won't be happy if she finds wet clothes in the hamper," he said, which was true, and Thomas knew firsthand. He'd come back from baseball practice once last spring, his pants wet and grass-stained from practicing the day after a rainstorm, and thrown his clothes directly into the hamper. Mom gagged when she pulled them out three days later.

So, here they stood: two skinny eleven-year-old boys in their underwear, unruly curly brown hair sweaty and damp and clinging to their foreheads, and an even skinnier eleven-year-old girl in a large shirt, with brown hair longer and rattier than her brothers'. The three of them lined up along the edge of the pool, toes wiggling above the water, the thick humid air and chlorine smell surrounding them.

One quick dip, and then back to bed all cooled off, body temperatures down. Simple biology.

"Ready?" Joey asked, though she didn't intend on waiting to see if they were. "One . . . two . . ."

"Hey! What are you doing out here!"

There was the sudden bright light of a flashlight

in her face, and Joey realized that no, she wouldn't be cooling down, and yes, she would be in big trouble. Thomas let out a loud shriek, and she heard Colton suck in a big breath of air, and Joey's chest felt tight—real tight—and maybe she got scared, maybe he surprised her too much, maybe it was just a reflex.

Because Joey responded the way she always did, the way that her moms both begged and yelled at her not to.

With her fists.

Just as quickly as he shouted at them, Joey turned and punched the security guard square in the belly. He fell directly into the pool, and Joey couldn't even enjoy the cool splash of the water as it hit her face.

Joey's moms were called, and so was the landlord, and it was one (maybe two) strikes too many, so close to the end of their lease.

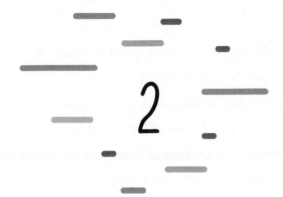

2

That was how the entire Sennett-Cooper family (minus Benny) ended up squashed together in a small motel room on Highway 36 up the road from their old apartment complex in Highlands, New Jersey. It had one king-sized bed and a cot that her moms had offered Joey, but it was lumpy and thin, and way less comfortable than the hard floor. Most of their things were in storage, and the rest were in the suitcases they had shoved against the far wall of the room.

Joey's mom wasn't talking to her, not really. It was a long week of anger, of Mom pausing, all tensed up, to count to ten every time someone complained about the lack of space, when they realized they had no control over the thermostat, when Benny declared he would be staying with his dad instead.

Joey, though, preferred Mom's anger to the concerned glances Mama kept giving her.

Joey was the recipient of one of those glances now. She was sitting on the floor next to the bed, extra blankets bunched up underneath her, and a pillow behind her. The boys kept rotating between who would share the bed with their moms and who would take the cot, but Joey was fine with staying on the floor. Mama was a cuddler. Four days after the pool incident, it was still too hot for such nonsense.

Mama was looking at Joey like she was going to scoop her up and cuddle her, regardless of the blame floating around for their lost apartment and how they hadn't found a good replacement yet.

"What?" Joey asked.

"You gotta start talking to us, Jo-Jo," Mama said. She ran a hand through her knotted hair, trying to pull those knots free.

Because the triplets shared half their DNA with Mama, Joey figured her own hair, as usual, was just as messy. It was easy to trace what the three of them had inherited from Mama. Mama's thick dark hair and bushy eyebrows, her brown eyes, her strong nose and cheekbones—the triplets had gotten all of that. The triplets and Mama could all roll their tongues and had sharply pointed widow's peaks on their foreheads. They all had unattached earlobes and their second toes were longer than the first.

Joey didn't know much about the donor that made up the other half of the triplets, but they looked like Mama, so it didn't really matter, and Joey didn't usually have to think about him all that much.

Except, she thought about him a lot lately. Especially when Mom was so mad, and Benny said he was leaving, and they were all cramped in a motel room—all because of Joey.

(Mom couldn't roll her tongue. She had blond hair with no widow's peak, and her earlobes were attached. All her toes were in nice descending-size order; Joey had looked at them last night as they dangled off the motel bed, a little too close to her face.)

"We can't help you if you don't tell us what you need," Mama continued, pulling Joey from her thoughts. "Your decisions lately are worrying me."

And there it was, the reason Joey couldn't help but wonder about the donor. Mama had been saying this sort of thing for months now, even more in the past week. The last time Joey had stolen Mama's phone to play a game on, she found all sorts of websites book-marked. Ones about *anger management*, and *therapy*, and *child psychiatrists*.

The incident with the security guard wasn't exactly the first. Mama was worried that it wouldn't be the last. Mom was fed up with all of it.

It was easy to dismiss the broken railing in the hallway stairwell of their apartment complex as an accident—even if Joey had knocked it right off the wall after getting mad at Thomas for not carrying his fair share of groceries up the three flights of stairs. It was easy to say "children will be children" when they got noise complaints from Joey's screaming fits—even if Mom said Joey was way too old to be throwing those kinds of temper tantrums.

There wasn't much they could say about this, though, and Mom didn't seem to even want to try making excuses.

Joey knew all this, of course, because there weren't many ways to argue without being overheard in a small motel room. Even if they only whisper-yelled about it.

"She's just always so *angry*," Mama had said. "Luka said it's getting worse in school. She's so mean to the other kids."

"She has nothing to be angry about, Becca. Motel room aside, she has a pretty good life, if you ask me," Mom had replied.

But Mama tried, just like she always did. "If we could just get her to slow down and *breathe*. Which is why I think therapy could be beneficial. She could learn coping strategies, have someone to actually talk to."

"I love you, but forgive me for not thinking that *breathing* is the issue here. And she knows she can talk to us."

"Then talk to her, Steph."

"I will. Okay? I will."

That was last night's argument, anyway. Joey assumed there'd be more of *that*, just like Mama assumed there'd be more *incidents*.

"Mama, I think my pants are too small," Colton said as he came out of the bathroom. It was true. They hit above his ankles.

"You grew again?" Mom said from where she was currently spraying detangler into Thomas's hair. Mom had thin, straight blond hair, the kind of hair where she could climb out of bed, run a hand through it, and be good for the rest of the day.

Those sorts of differences usually didn't cross Joey's mind, but she couldn't stop staring at Mom's hair now.

Mom glanced down at Thomas's pants. "You, too?"

"Just a little," Thomas said.

The boys were an entire head taller than Joey these days. She didn't usually think about that, either. About how even though the triplets were supposed to be the same, Joey actually wasn't. Not really. Not like Colton and Thomas.

"Sorry," Colton said.

"Not your fault, babe, but I'll ask Benny if he has any old pairs he can bring over until we can buy you two new ones. Sound good?" Mom asked.

The stuffy motel room got quiet at the mention of Benny.

"Is Benny coming back soon?" Joey quietly asked.

Benny shared half his DNA with Mom, but none with the triplets. The other half of his DNA came from Luka, who was Mom's ex-husband—and the triplets' gym teacher at the middle school.

Joey's grandma referred to their family's situation as "very modern."

It usually didn't matter, because Benny lived with them, and Benny called Mama *Mama*, too, even though he was already three when their moms met.

But Benny didn't hesitate to leave them when Joey got them thrown out of the apartment. "I'm not staying in a motel, I'm staying with Dad," he'd said, because he had that option. He hadn't stopped by the motel once.

"Luka was gracious enough to spare us another night of takeout and invited us over for dinner this weekend. We'll see Benny then," Mom said. She waved the hairbrush in Joey's direction, changing the subject. She didn't like that Benny left, either. "Come let me try and get those tangles out."

"It's fine," Joey said, running her fingers through her curls, getting snagged on a knot on the way down.

"Just let me fix it."

"I said it's *fine*," Joey snapped.

The room suddenly felt even smaller, even stuffier, as Thomas went completely still, and Colton got super interested in something inside of his backpack, and Mama's sigh was *so loud* in the much too quiet room.

Mom chucked the hairbrush onto the dresser with a clang. That seemed extra loud, too. "Fine. Go to school a mess. I don't care."

"Steph," Mama said, sighing again.

"Just forget it. We need to get going anyway. Gotta get this herd off to school before I'm late for work," Mom said. She was dressed in brown, ready to start her day delivering UPS packages.

Mama did most of her work at home from her laptop, but she had been walking to the coffee shop down the road the past four days. The motel had crappy wi-fi.

The boys sounded like an actual herd as they gathered their backpacks to meet Mom at the door. Joey gathered her things a little more quietly.

"Jo-Jo," Mama gently said from the bed, holding out a hand. "Come give me a hug."

Joey wasn't a cuddler like Mama.

Though maybe that wasn't true. Because when she leaned into Mama's arms, letting Mama basically pull her onto the bed and into her lap, Joey didn't mind, not even a little, as her mama's arms grew tighter around her. She rested her head on Mama's shoulder, and it felt easier to breathe.

"Have a good day at school," Mama whispered right into Joey's ear.

Joey knew she really meant *be good at school, please.* "Okay."

Mom told Joey to sit in the front seat of the car, as the boys, all long limbs and torsos, filed into the back. Joey, by sheer size alone, was usually unfairly stuck in that backseat, so it wasn't exactly a surprise when her mom pulled up to the front of their charter school and reached for Joey's arm, stopping her before she could even take her seatbelt off.

"Hang back a sec, Joey."

The boys exchanged glances as they said their goodbyes to Mom and climbed out of the car. They walked slowly, hovering around the school's front lawn, waiting on Joey without actually waiting.

Joey appreciated that. She didn't have any real friends here anymore besides her brothers.

Joey sighed and waited for Mom to talk. She shouldn't have snapped this morning. She was on thin ice with her moms already, and Joey somehow always made it worse.

Do not get mad, Joey told herself. *Mom gets so angry when you get mad during a lecture.* Mom had a lot of practice giving lectures. Mama, on the other hand, tended to hug instead of yell while doling out punishments.

Joey looked down at her hands, folded tightly together in her lap, so tightly her knuckles turned a little white. Her mom reached out to cup Joey's cheek, which she knew meant Mom wanted Joey to look at her.

So Joey turned to look at her.

Her mom's eyes were different than the rest of them—swirling blues and greens—which Joey had seen a million times before but was mesmerized by now.

"I love you, Little Growl," Mom said, using the nickname Joey had loved when she was little but wasn't too sure about these days. "You know that, right?"

Joey nodded. She knew that. Mostly.

There were different ways to make a family; Joey's mom was her mom even though Joey and her brothers were made from Mama and a donor and not from Mom at all. There was the legal paperwork, of course, which was tangible and real, regardless of the fact that Joey had never actually seen it. It was there, in a folder somewhere with the other important documents her moms kept safe.

(Joey had started thinking about that paperwork since they packed up to leave for the motel. She needed to see it, to understand it fully and completely, to know exactly what it meant.)

And then, of course, love also made a family.

Lately, though, Joey couldn't help but wonder if that love had limits. She wondered if she would eventually reach those limits. She got in fights at school. She got in fights at home. She got them all thrown out of their apartment.

Benny could choose to leave when things got messy. How easy would it be for anyone else to?

Mom tugged lightly at the tip of Joey's tangled hair. "Think you can do me a favor today? Be nice to someone who isn't your brother, alright? I need you to rein it in. Despite the fact that you seem determined to prove otherwise, I raised you, so I *know* you're a sweet kid."

Joey scrunched up her nose.

"Don't give me that face," Mom said, reaching over to tickle Joey's side. "You're sweet and you know it and

17

I really, really need you to prove to the world that you can laugh and smile."

She didn't stop tickling and Joey squirmed and fought but couldn't help but laugh. Soft, quiet giggles she couldn't hold in no matter how hard she tried.

"Stop, Mom, stop!" she said between laughter.

Her mom stopped, smile big on her face. "I love that sound. I miss it."

Joey felt herself blushing. She didn't know why she was mean to the other girls in school. She didn't know why she felt better after hitting something (or someone). She didn't know why she couldn't stop herself from doing it.

She wished there was a way to figure it all out.

"Can I go now?" Joey asked.

Mom sighed, but nodded. "Yeah, get out of here. Go learn something, will you?"

Joey unbuckled and climbed out. Before she shut the door, she looked at her mom's face, really looked. Mom's blue-green eyes were searching Joey's brown ones. They looked so tired.

"Love you, too, Mom," Joey said, and closed the door.

3

Since Colton and Thomas were identical, they were always separated each school year. And since Navasink Charter was small—there were only two sixth-grade classes—Joey was usually stuck with one of them. She was relieved she had been paired with Colton instead of Thomas this year.

Joey had asked Mama how Colton and Thomas were identical once she was old enough to understand. They used to spend Mama's lunch break together, watching the Discovery Channel or Animal Planet. Joey had always loved watching animal shows; when she was little, she used to impersonate the animals, hopping around like a frog or walking on all fours, growling loudly like one of the big cats.

They were watching a show on lions in which a lioness had just given birth to a litter of three, just like Mama. "Are all those cubs the same? How come Thomas and Colton are the same and I'm not?"

"We talked about in vitro fertilization, do you remember that?" Mama had replied, as she curled up on the couch, pulling Joey into her lap. "They create the embryos in a petri dish, and then put them in my uterus to grow. To care for."

"That's so weird."

Mama had laughed. "That's perfectly natural, Jo-Jo! But trying to get pregnant that way can be really hard. So they didn't just try with one embryo—we tried two."

"But there are three of us," Joey said.

"Both embryos worked," Mama said, and Joey couldn't help but feel proud of both herself *and* her brothers, even though they really had nothing to do with it. "One of them split into two. Two identical twins. And you, fraternal."

Joey loved hearing Mama explain it. "So the boys are the same. And then there's me."

"Exactly," Mama said. "And then there's you."

Since Colton and Thomas looked, well, *identical*, and teachers got confused (even though Colton and Thomas were *nothing* alike, besides their shared looks), they were separated on purpose. Joey thought it must be nice, sometimes, to not have a sibling in the same class who could tattle on her if she didn't do her homework or who she'd be forced to see all day if she was mad at them. But that was a privilege for one of the boys every year, never her, and at least Colton was one of her best friends.

Well. He was her *only* best friend. She didn't really have anyone else, anymore.

Colton was currently on the basketball court in the school gymnasium, playing a game of kickball with the rest of their gym class. Their teacher, Luka (who they were supposed to call Coach Cooper in school, but only Thomas ever remembered to do so), was pitching the ball. Colton was on second base.

Joey was on the bleachers. She wasn't allowed to participate in gym for the rest of the month because of an incident a couple weeks ago with a soccer ball and Danny Carter's bruised collarbone.

The punishment probably would have been worse,

but sometimes it worked to her benefit that the gym teacher had once been married to Joey's mom—even if that was super weird to think about.

Aubrey Massie, who was standing closest to the bleachers on first base, kept turning around to stare at Joey. Joey scowled at her, using her fingers to make the shape of whiskers next to her nose. Aubrey quickly looked away. *Good.* Aubrey had been the first one to sell Joey out about Danny's collarbone. Joey had been calling her a rat ever since.

Luka, who from the look on his face had seen the whole exchange, motioned at the textbooks sitting closed next to Joey.

She was supposed to be doing her homework.

(Which she was, mostly. But besides defending her honor, she had been making faces at Colton. He got *so mad* at distractions during gym class. He played to win.)

"Your brother looks like he needs to do some of your mama's breathing exercises."

Joey had been too busy pretending to give Colton the finger (not *really* giving him the finger—Luka would *not* be pleased) to notice that Layla was suddenly sitting next to her. Which was weird, because back when they were best friends, Joey had *always* noticed Layla.

"You and Thomas are the only ones who think Mama's meditation stuff actually works," Joey said, finally opening her notebook to start working. "What're you doing here?"

"I was up way too late because we found a new relative on my mom's ancestry account, like from the 1600s. I think he was a real Viking! So anyway, I was researching them and completely forgot to pack my gym clothes," Layla said, shrugging. "You know how Coach Cooper is."

Layla and her mom had been tracing their family tree for over a year now. It was easy, because Layla was her mom and dad's biological daughter and they could simply draw a line to Layla's grandparents, and their parents, and so on, to find out where they were born and how they lived and who they were.

Layla had wanted to trace Joey's family, too, but at the time it sounded exhausting. Would they just trace Mama's side? Would they do Mom's, too, even though they weren't actually Joey's biological ancestors? It was a little too complicated.

Still, she almost let Layla do it anyway because she liked making Layla happy.

But the fact that she really liked making Layla happy was the whole problem in the first place, so Joey didn't ask Layla about her new relative.

Joey didn't say anything and focused instead on Layla's favorite purple Vans. She had on a purple sweatshirt to match and was tugging on the strings, messing up the hood. Her black hair was tucked inside of it.

"How much longer are you out for?" Layla asked. She leaned her head forward to meet Joey's eyes, smiling. Joey—who was still staring, trying to decide if Layla's nose was more like her mom's or her dad's (her dad's, definitely her dad's . . . but also maybe her mom's)—quickly looked away. She hated the way her hands felt sweaty.

"We don't have to do this," Joey said, slamming her notebook shut before wiping her hands on her jeans.

"Do what?" Layla asked. "We're just—"

"*Go away*, Layla," Joey snapped. "You're just gonna get me in trouble anyway."

There were shouts from the basketball court, followed by Colton yelling, "In your face!" Joey looked over to find him with the kickball in one of his hands, punching the air with the other. Eric Byers, who had kicked the ball right into Colton's hands, didn't look all that thrilled.

The game continued, and Joey toyed with the edge of her notebook, refusing to look back in Layla's direction. She had been here before, again and again and again, and she didn't want to see the look on Layla's face.

She had pretty much memorized it, anyway.

"Whatever, Joey," Layla finally said. She got up and started walking down the bleachers, away from Joey, before stopping and turning around. "I don't know what's wrong with you, but the least you could do is not make it weird for Colton and me. *He's* still my best friend."

Layla moved to the other side of the bleachers, five rows down, pretty much as far away from Joey as she could go without sitting on the gym floor. Joey watched the back of Layla's head, the purple hood of her sweatshirt all bunched up when she tugged at the strings.

Layla didn't know what was wrong with Joey.

Joey didn't know either. She didn't know what made her want to yell, what made her throw the soccer ball as hard as she could at Danny when he was standing right in front of her. She didn't know what made her kick her brothers awake to go jump into a closed pool in the middle of the night. She didn't know what made her hit her brothers when they made her mad, didn't know what made her scream and scream and *scream* at her moms until her throat hurt, when they wouldn't listen.

But Joey knew exactly why she wouldn't talk to Layla.

It just made things a lot easier.

4

Joey didn't like family dinners. Thomas and Mama both had this laugh that could rival a donkey, and Mom and Colton yelled their words when they got excited about something, and there was always this dull ringing in Joey's ears when she had to sit, surrounded by all of them, as food was passed around the table. Colton scraped his teeth against his fork every time he took a bite, and Mom clanked her teeth against her glass every time she took a drink, and it was all just a little too much. Always.

Tonight, though, Joey would tolerate it with a smile on her face.

Because Benny was here.

(*Benny* was actually her favorite brother.)

They were at Luka's place, sitting around his small table. He'd made a lasagna, and it was kind of burnt; the top layer was too hard to eat. Joey was sitting next to Benny, trying to figure out if she should say she was sorry for getting them thrown out of their apartment, or what she could say to make him come home, or to ask him if, when they found a place to live, he would come with them or stay here.

"This is delicious, Luka. Thank you," Mama said. She and Luka didn't always get along, but Mama was *always* nice.

Mom laughed in response. Joey had no idea how she was ever married to Luka. They bickered with each other on a good day.

"What?" Luka said. "Why are you laughing like that? I cook a meal out of the kindness of my heart and you *laugh*?"

"No, you're right, I'm sorry," Mom said, pulling the burnt layer off the lasagna. "We really appreciate it. Especially since I get to see my oldest baby tonight!" She wrapped an arm around Benny, her cheek squishing against his as she leaned in close for a hug.

"I've been gone for, like, barely a week, Mom," Benny said.

"Can I have the Parmesan cheese?" Thomas asked.

"Yeah, well. A week too many," Mom said. "It doesn't matter anyway. We'll find a new place and be out of that motel as soon as humanly possible."

"I don't know, Steph. If he stays here, you can look for a smaller place. Might be easier," Luka chimed in. "It's been good for us to spend some time together. He'll be off to college before we know it."

"Yeah, well, it's not really your decision, Luka," Mom said.

"Can we not?" Benny chimed in. "There's barely any room in that motel, I have an entire room to myself here. Let's not make this into some custody thing, okay? Besides, I'm seventeen, it should be *my* decision."

"Let's just take a moment here, yeah? Have a nice family dinner?" Mama said, leaning over to gently grasp Benny's arm. "This is a weird situation, and everyone is a little tense."

"The cheese," Thomas said again. "Can someone pass it to me?"

"Fine. Let's just change the subject, then," Benny said.

Joey pushed her fork around her plate. This was all her fault, anyway.

"When does hockey start?" Colton asked.

"First weekend of October," Benny said. "So, soon. You should come to the rink to practice with me. Maybe get you ready for Dad's new team."

"Colton, seriously!" Thomas said. "I want the cheese!"

"Jesus Christ, Thomas, *here!*" Joey reached across the table for the Parmesan cheese and threw it across the table at Thomas. It landed in his dish, sauce splattering and cheese sprinkling the air like a cloud of dust.

The table grew quiet. It was actually a relief to Joey's ears.

"You are excused, Joey," Mom said, her voice low and angry.

"I'm not done," Joey said.

"Yes. You are." Mom left no room for argument. "Go sit in the other room and wait for the rest of us to finish."

Right. That was the other reason Joey hated family dinners.

They always seemed to end early for her.

Colton was the first one to go looking for her, because he always did. Joey was in Benny's bedroom, sitting on his blue comforter with her knees pulled into her chest, her head resting against them. Joey always hated that when Benny would get in fights with their moms, he would threaten to come stay here.

"My house, my rules!" Mom would say.

"Then I'll go to Dad's," Benny would threaten. Sometimes, he would even follow through. For one painful month of Benny's freshman year of high school, he hadn't come home once after some big blowout with Mom over his ADHD medication.

"I know Thomas is annoying, but did you really have to throw that at him?" Colton said, and Joey felt the bed dip as he sat next to her. "Dinner got weird after you left."

"Dinner was already weird. Besides, Mom didn't have to make me leave."

"*You* didn't have to throw the cheese at him!"

31

Joey didn't want to do this. She didn't want to start arguing and then not be able to stop. "Is dinner over? I wanted to spend time with Benny."

"They're just cleaning up now. Thomas made the mistake of offering to help, so I bounced. Hey, I bet if you go help, you'll get brownie points with Mom," Colton said.

Joey made a face. "Hey, Colton? Is it my fault things are weird with you and Layla, too?"

Colton shrugged.

"You can still be friends with her, you know," Joey said. "I don't care."

"We *are* still friends. We just don't know why you're not anymore, so it's weird to invite her over to hang. Not that there's room for friends in the motel anyway," Colton said. He tucked his hair behind his ear, squinting at Joey. She didn't like the way that felt—he only got squinty when he was concentrating hard, and she didn't want him to see her too closely. "Do you not like Layla anymore? Did she do something?"

"Why does it matter? Is she, like, your girlfriend?" Joey only said it to deflect, but it made her stomach clench anyway.

"No, she's just my best friend," Colton said,

and then shoved Joey for extra emphasis. "Don't be annoying."

Joey tried to hold back a smile. "Don't shove me," she said, and promptly shoved him back.

So he shoved her again. "You know she's the only person in school who can put up with you."

"Shut up," Joey said, and pushed him harder.

Colton grabbed at her sleeve and pulled her to the floor, pinning her down.

That was when they both started laughing.

They'd been doing this since they were little, tackling and wrestling and rolling around over their toys that were always scattered around the living room, no matter how much Mama begged them to clean up after themselves. Mom used to join them. She'd pick one of them up high into the air and pretend to body-slam them on the floor, placing them down gently and tickling them to mercy, as one of the other triplets, most often Joey, would climb up on Mom's back to try and bring her down with them.

Mom didn't wrestle with them anymore. Joey wished she still did.

Joey wiggled out of Colton's grasp and pushed him down and climbed on top of him, and he reached his arm around her to shove her head into Benny's worn bedroom rug. "Say 'uncle'!" Colton said.

Joey would never. She used her free hand, the one that wasn't pinned underneath her body, to reach for Colton's face. She hooked a finger into his mouth and his nose. "Ew, stop!" Colton said, cracking up.

Joey managed to wiggle herself free and knelt on top of Colton's back. He couldn't move, and she was going to win and—

The bedroom door opened. Joey and Colton froze where they were, tangled together, with deer-wide eyes.

But it was only Benny. "Really, you two?" he asked, reaching for them both and tackling them to the ground, effectively ending the wrestling match.

"Get off, you big lug," Joey said, and Benny rolled off the two of them, moving to sit on the floor against his bed instead. Joey and Colton joined on either side of him.

"Or what? You'll throw cheese at my head, too?" Benny asked.

He had a hole in one of his socks, and Joey found herself focusing on that instead of his face. "I didn't throw it at his head."

"Mom got pretty mad."

"Mom's always mad at me," Joey said. *"Always."*

It was that anger that made Joey think more and more lately about the paperwork, the one that said Joey was Mom's daughter. Now that they were in the motel, though, finding it was probably an impossible task. For all Joey knew, it was currently trapped in storage.

Speaking of . . . "Are you gonna stay here even after we leave the motel?" Joey asked.

Benny shrugged. "I don't know. Might make things easier."

"For who? You?"

"For everyone! But I'm sure I'll come back, and maybe just stay here more often," Benny said. "That landlord was a jerk, you know. He didn't have to throw us out like that."

Colton snorted. "Mama said we're lucky he didn't call the cops."

Which was news to Joey. *Though*, a voice in Joey's head told her, *maybe we wouldn't have had to leave the apartment if cops came and took you away.* "When did she say that?"

"Listen, I was thinking," Benny interrupted. He

patted Joey on the thigh, which was something Mom did a lot, too. The thought made Joey's stomach clench again. A reminder that Benny and Mom were a pair.

Don't get mad, Joey told herself.

"You know the hockey team my dad's starting at your school? You might've been too young to remember, but when I was having trouble focusing, because of my ADHD, that's when my dad got me started playing," Benny explained. "And, I don't know. I think you should give it a try. Could help you get some of that aggression out, you know?"

"I thought it was a boys' team?" Colton asked.

Benny shrugged. "I'm pretty sure it's school policy that if they don't offer a girls' version of a sport, they have to let girls try out for the boys' ones. I'm sure it'd be cool with my dad, he'd stick up for you. But maybe it'll make things . . . easier? At home I mean."

Joey felt her cheeks flush. Benny was telling her that things were hard at home, because of her. That maybe he wouldn't come home . . . because of her.

But what was hockey going to do? Even if it got her aggression out . . . Joey got her aggression out in little ways all the time. She felt better for a hot second after she threw the Parmesan at Thomas. She almost smiled when it landed right in his dish. That didn't keep the feelings from coming back, though. They always did. She always wanted to hit or yell or throw something again. "Hockey's not gonna help," Joey said.

"You're going to have to figure out what will, Little Growl," Benny said.

Or else, what? He sounded so much like Mom sometimes. "Mom says I have a good life. I have no right to be this angry."

"Mama used to make me do breathing exercises, expecting that to fix everything. Moms don't have *all* the answers," Benny said. "So, think about it. I can talk to my dad for you, if you want. At the very least, you might end up really liking hockey. You, too, Colton. I still remember how much fun my very first game was, and how excited Mom was in the stands."

"Mom goes nuts in the stands." Colton laughed. "Mama has to, like, pull her back down sometimes when she starts standing up and yelling. Oh, man, and she hated that one ref, remember?"

Benny laughed, too. "Oh, God, yeah, tell me about it. But she loves it so much, I just try and ignore her."

Mom *did* love hockey. She met Benny's dad at a Devils game. She was rooting for the opposite team, and Benny's dad bet that if the Devils won, she had to go on a date with him.

The Devils lost. She went on a date with him anyway.

Maybe hockey wouldn't help Joey's issues. Benny's ADHD wasn't the same as whatever was making her so angry.

But maybe it would make Benny remember the things he liked about Joey. Maybe it would make Joey's mom happy, too.

"Just think about it, okay?" Benny said.

Joey nodded. She had to. Because in the back of her mind, she was thinking about the limits of love, about Benny's bedroom at his dad's, Mom's face at dinner, and how maybe, just maybe, blood really *was* thicker than water.

"Okay," Joey said. "I'll think about it."

5

Joey, who always sat in the last row, in the back
corner of the classroom, was leaning back in her seat,
impatiently waiting for Mr. Hoover to *spit it out already*.
They had been in science class for, like, ten entire minutes and he was drawing this whole thing out.

Torturing Joey, if you asked her.

Next to Joey, where he always sat, Colton had his
chin resting on his desk. "I hope it's something cool.
Like, tornados or tsunamis. Not something boring,
like *plants*," he whispered.

"Excuse you, plants are *awesome*. They have their
own biological makeup just like we do, Colton," Layla
said from the desk on the other side of him. Her leg

was bouncing. "Did you know you can trace back their origins, too, just like with people?"

"What? Like, a tree's family tree?"

"Not exactly."

"Will you two *shush*?" Joey said.

"I'm so excited," Layla said, ignoring Joey. "I spent all last week trying to get everyone to vote my way."

Mr. Hoover was their youngest teacher, which by default made him the coolest. But what really set him apart from any other science teachers Joey had ever had was that he was letting *them* decide, both of the sixth-grade classes, what they studied for an entire unit this year. It was the one thing they had all looked forward to about going into sixth grade.

Thomas's class was going to be learning earth sciences—earthquakes and volcanoes and tsunamis—for the next couple months. Joey and Colton's class was going to find out now what they'd be doing.

Please don't be boring, please don't be boring.

Mr. Hoover had had them all rate a bunch of topics, from favorite to least favorite. Joey didn't have a favorite, but she made sure to point out all the ones she found super boring. Layla instructed Colton to write down her choice as his top one. If Joey was a good friend, she would probably have written down Layla's choice as her top, too.

"You all ranked your topics with very nice consideration, though some of you took the time to actually think these out a little more than others," Mr. Hoover said, raising his eyebrows at Joey. She fought the urge to interrupt him and say, *Yeah yeah yeah we know, get on with it already.*

"Some topics came close, but we did have a clear winner. So without further ado"—Mr. Hoover did everything with *so much ado*—"we're going to be focusing on genetics and genealogy—"

"Yes!" Layla said, jumping a little out of her seat.

Mr. Hoover laughed. "Which obviously pleases Layla."

Joey sighed. Of *course* it did. Layla's lineage was straightforward.

Joey's lineage was a weird puzzle missing a bunch of pieces.

So much for sixth grade being better than learning about the world's most boring ecosystems. At least it was just for one unit.

"I can see by some of your faces you're already a little worried," Mr. Hoover said. "But, listen, rest assured

I'm not just interested in your genetics for this class. A lot of you come from different backgrounds, have different types of families, all of which are valid. Which is why I want to talk about environmental factors, too. Nature versus nurture. Our genes, our choices."

Colton raised his hand but spoke at the same time (which effectively negated the point of raising his hand in the first place, but whatever). "But that doesn't make sense. You can't talk about genes like we have any choices. That's kind of the point, right?"

"Yeah, but not everything comes from genes," Layla said. "Like, sure, you can trace a lot of things through DNA, but don't you have things in common with your mom?"

Joey scowled at her, ignoring the blush she felt creep up the back of her neck. "We don't share any DNA with our mom."

"Yeah, but you both have a temper," Colton said.

Mr. Hoover, still laughing, held up his hands. "Alright, alright. I don't mean to stir up a family fight here, but Layla raises a point. Are traits inherited, or are they a result of environmental interactions? Or are they *both*? That's what I want us to think about. That's what we're going to be focusing on for this first unit.

Understanding the difference between nature, meaning our genes, and nurture, meaning the environment in which we live and the things that happen to us. And looking at the role played by both nature *and* nurture in defining who we are and what it means to be human."

Joey sat back in her seat, fists balled up at her sides. She didn't want to think about any of this. She didn't want to think of all of the ways that she was different. From her brothers, the identical twins. From her mom and Benny.

Though, maybe she should.

Maybe if she tried to sort out her own DNA, her molecules and nucleotides, at the very basic, black-and-white level, she could figure out what it was that made her . . . *her.* The things that made her so angry, the things that made them have to live in a stupid motel room and made Benny leave.

It might be the only way to fix things so that her family didn't give up on her.

~~~~•

Speaking of that stupid hotel room, Joey was going to scream if Thomas didn't stop pulling his clothes out of the suitcases, leaving her clothes all balled up and wrinkled and impossible to find. "Thomas, I hate you! I can't find anything!" Joey said, throwing his clothes at him.

Thomas ducked. "It's not just me! Colton does it, too!"

"Don't touch my stuff!"

"Rein it in, Joey," Mom said from her spot on the bed next to Mama, as they watched the clunky motel TV.

"This is so dumb, we should unpack," Joey said. "I can't find *anything*!"

"Not a chance, Little Growl, we're not staying here much longer," Mom said, picking up the remote to turn the volume down. "Mama and I are going to look at a place this weekend."

"So let me unpack enough stuff until then!"

"Hey, come sit and relax with us, Joey," Mama chimed in, patting the bed next to her. Colton was sprawled out at the bottom of the bed, and Thomas was on the floor.

"Oh, Mom, can you drive us to Aubrey's party on Saturday?" Thomas asked.

"What party?" Joey asked. This was the first time

Joey was hearing about it, even though Aubrey was in classes with her and Colton, not Thomas.

"Her birthday party," Thomas said, as if that answered anything.

"What time?" Mom asked. "I can probably take and pick you up around my work shift."

"Layla said all the girls are sleeping over," Colton added. "So Joey's probably gonna stay."

So, Colton knew about the party, too. "Aubrey never told me about any party."

Her brothers exchanged glances with one another. "Maybe she didn't get a chance to tell you about it yet?" Thomas said.

"You're a terrible liar, Thomas," Joey snapped. It was true though. He was just like Mama in that way. They all were. "Just say it. I wasn't invited."

"Well, wait a minute, Jo-Jo, maybe—"

Joey didn't want Mama's kind words or made-up excuses on Aubrey's behalf. They meant nothing. Aubrey meant nothing. She was just a girl in their class, and it meant nothing. "I don't care. It doesn't matter. Aubrey Massie is a rat, and I wouldn't go to her boring party if I was invited anyway."

"We don't need to go either," Thomas said hesitantly.

"I already told Layla I'm going," Colton said.

"I don't *care* what you and Layla do, Colton!"

"Hey!" Mom said, reaching for Joey's arm and pulling her toward the bed. "Come here. Come relax and sit with us."

"Deep breaths, Joey," Mama added.

Even Mom rolled her eyes at that. Joey leaned against the bed, letting Mom's arm wrap around her.

"How about this," Mama said from the other side of the bed. "Mom will take the boys to the party, and you and I can spend the day together, okay? Just us. Some Mama and Joey time. How's that sound? We haven't done anything just the two of us in ages, not since you started school and I lost my lunch-break buddy."

"Oh, I'm a little jealous," Mom said, leaning over to kiss Mama on the cheek. "Where's my one-on-one Mama time?"

"Gross," Colton said.

"Excuse you!" Mom threw one of the pillows over at Colton's head. "There is nothing gross about your mothers' love for one another! I will kiss and cuddle her all I want!" To emphasize her point, Mom pressed her face against Mama's cheek to kiss it again and wrapped her arms around Mama, holding her tightly.

Mama turned to kiss Mom on the lips before focusing back on Joey. "What do you say, Jo-Jo? You and me on Saturday?"

Joey sighed. It wasn't like it mattered anyway. "Fine."

6

That night, when Joey was supposed to be asleep, she overheard Mom and Mama talking about the party. She couldn't wait to be out of this stupid motel so she wouldn't have to hear them talk about her anymore. "I mean, is it really a surprise?" Mom said. "She's been acting out. She's mean to those other girls. They're going to start being wary of her."

"I just hate it. Being excluded clearly hurt her. I don't like any of this," Mama said.

"I mean, can you blame them, though?" Mom said. "Sometimes I'm wary of her, too."

Colton must have noticed Joey was awake and listening, though. He climbed out of the cot, feet heavy and loud, to go to the bathroom, stopping their moms from saying anything more.

Saturday afternoon, when the boys got ready for Aubrey's birthday party, Mama dug in the suitcases for some of her and Joey's heavier clothing. September was changing to fall, and the weather, while still warm, was starting to change, too. "Here, wear this one."

"This is Mom's," Joey said, taking the oversized old Blackhawks sweatshirt and putting it on. Mama wore a deep royal blue sweater that hung off her shoulder, like something on a runway. Joey's moms' styles were so different from one another.

"Why do I need a sweatshirt anyway?" Joey asked. "What're we doing? Can't we just watch TV like we used to?"

"I think you've been cooped up in this small room for too long and could use some fresh air, experience *real* nature," Mama said.

Both Mom and Colton laughed at that.

Joey probably would have laughed, too, if it weren't happening to her. Mama wasn't vegetarian, but that didn't stop her from ordering vegan from the restaurant down the street from their old apartment. She made sure to bring a diffuser to the motel room and spent every night trying new scent blends to help them all "relax" and "find inner peace." She did yoga on Sundays and was a big fan of telling Joey and her brothers to "just breathe" any time they got worked up about something.

Mama was an instructional designer who spent most of her days on her laptop building online classes for colleges, but deep down, she was basically a hippie.

"I don't need fresh air," Joey said.

"Let's go boys, I can't be late to work, and you shouldn't be late to this party," Mom said, gathering up the boys. She reached over to kiss Joey on the side of her head. "Good luck with the fresh outdoors, Little Growl."

Mama took Joey to the wooded hills of Hartshorne Park, which was right by the ocean and only about a ten-minute walk from home (so, of course, Mama made them walk). It was windier down by the water, and Joey pulled the hood of Mom's sweatshirt up over her head and pulled on the strings to make the face hole smaller—which reminded her of Layla, who was hanging out with Colton and Thomas and probably the rest of her classmates at Aubrey's party.

"Keep up, Jo-Jo, you're falling behind," Mama

said, pointing at the trail marker telling them to turn. They were going higher and higher, and Joey's legs were starting to ache.

"This definitely isn't as fun as a party, if you're trying to make me feel better."

"Fresh air is good, and us getting some time alone is even better," Mama said. "I've been wanting to talk to you. It's been tough to have any space lately."

"Yeah, I know." Joey frowned. "If you want to talk about how the motel is my fault, I know that already."

"That's not . . ." Mama stopped walking with a sigh. "Okay. Yes, that's what I want to talk about. But not the motel. Am I happy you punched a security guard? No. I understand he startled you, and you didn't mean to get violent. And your brothers were there with you. You don't need to take on all the blame here, Jo. But that doesn't change the fact that you've been acting out lately, and we need to figure this out. I'm worried about you."

Joey looked down at her toes. "Do you ever . . ." She dug the toe of her shoe into the dirt, kicking a rock out from where it was stuck in the earth.

"What?" Mama asked, when Joey didn't say anything else. "You know you can talk to me."

"Do you ever get really mad, for no reason? Like you need to scream or you can't breathe?" Joey asked. She had never seen Mama get all that mad. But Mama was her closest link to understanding her genetics. She and Mama weren't all that alike; this walk proved that, since Mama was enjoying it so much. But Joey felt like, regardless of their differences, Mama was a roadmap to half of who Joey was.

"Is that how you feel?" Mama asked.

Joey hated when Mama answered questions with a question. She started walking again, following the trail, with Mama slowing her speed to fall in step beside her. "I don't know," Joey lied. "But do you?"

"I think sometimes I get really frustrated. Like, if you and your brothers are fighting, or if Mom just throws her dirty dishes in the sink and leaves them there for me to clean even though she knows that drives me nuts. It makes me want to yell sometimes." The trail took them into a wooded area, and Mama pulled a hair tie off her wrist and handed it to Joey. "Pull your hair up, in case there are ticks."

"You don't ever just yell though, even if you want to," Joey said, taking the hair tie and doing as she was told. She took a deep breath before softly asking, "Have you ever hit anyone?"

"No," Mama said, without hesitation. "That I've never done."

Joey fell quiet as they continued walking. The crunch of the dirt and leaves under their feet and the crash of the waves down below was probably soothing for Mama. There were even birds chirping, like music from nature or something. Joey tried to listen to it, tried to let it relax her like she knew it was probably relaxing Mama. That was why Mama liked the outdoors. She said it was peaceful. Joey tried, but just . . . didn't get it.

Joey watched as Mama's hair blew in the wind. It was close to the same as Joey's and her brothers', but wavier, and just a little darker. "What did the donor look like?"

She hesitated, stunned that she had asked the question. No one ever said she or her brothers couldn't wonder about their donor—her moms always said it was okay to ask and be curious—but still, no one ever *actually* talked about it. Except occasionally just to ask whether or not a particular quality came from Mama or not.

And they never dwelled on that *or not*.

Mama paused, mid-step, before continuing. "The donor?"

"You know," Joey said. "For me and the boys. The donor. The in vitro."

"Oh. Well. He, the donor, shared some characteristics with Mom," Mama said, looking down at her feet as they walked. "Why do you ask?"

"Nothing, no reason," Joey was quick to answer.

"It's okay to ask," Mama said.

"I know. It's fine. Just wondering," Joey answered.

They came to the top of the hill, a clearing that looked out high above the shore town below them, the ocean, and the beach. Joey watched the waves crash against the rocks and the boats out on the water.

"Wow. I never get tired of this view," Mama said.

Joey looked out at that horizon, at how long it stretched and how small everything below them looked. She felt bigger than all of it; bigger than every single person down there, and much, much farther away. She could scream from up here, and they would only hear the echo. She could scream from up here, as long and as loud as she wanted, and no one would tell her to stop.

She took a deep breath, and felt the fresh, cool sea-salted air filling her lungs. She thought about it, about screaming. About shouting as loud as she could until her chest hurt.

Which was when Mama wrapped her arms around Joey's shoulders, and hugged her close. "It's beautiful here."

Joey exhaled that breath, quietly releasing it.

She couldn't scream here, with Mama, who never had the impulse to shout, to hit, to be angry.

Which meant the reason that Joey wanted to scream, that Joey wanted to fight and yell and hit, came from the other half of Joey's DNA.

7

Mr. Hoover was passing out worksheets (Mr. Hoover loved a worksheet) as he asked, "What does the phrase 'it's genetic' mean?"

"It means it comes from your genes and DNA," Layla called out, which made Joey roll her eyes.

Joey really didn't want to fill out a worksheet. She just knew she was going to have to answer questions about her biological parents and how their specific physical traits created Joey's. Dad's genes plus Mom's genes equals Baby's genes. Who had dominant genes, and who had recessive. Joey and Colton wouldn't be able to really answer the questions, and neither would

Danny Carter, who barely knew his dad, or Carlos Nelson, who was adopted.

Mom's genes plus Mama's genes wasn't exactly scientifically possible, and didn't equal anything, let alone Joey.

"Thanks, Layla, but raise your hand, okay?" Mr. Hoover said. "I want you all to think about what traits you *think* are genetically determined. I'm not just talking about eye and hair color—I know you all know this by now. I want you to think a little deeper. What about personalities?"

He handed Joey one of the worksheets. She looked down at it, realizing it wasn't a dominant and recessive gene chart after all. It was a list of traits, with two columns next to them that said *Genes* and *Environment*. Joey read the list: blue eyes, enjoys bungee jumping, six feet tall, red hair, IQ of 150, smokes cigarettes, weighs 250 pounds, has cancer, alcoholic, has depression.

"Take a look at this list," Mr. Hoover continued. "And think about which of those traits listed you think are genetic, determined by your DNA, and which of those traits are learned or environmentally influenced."

"They all are from DNA," Joey called out. "Aren't they?"

Mr. Hoover tapped his finger on the worksheet on her desk. "That's what we're going to figure out these next few weeks."

Joey looked back down at the sheet. Next to her, Colton said, "There's no way Mama would ever go bungee-jumping. *I* totally would."

Layla leaned over to chime in, "Your mama might not, but I bet your mom would. Neither of them would let *you*, though."

Joey ignored them. She was too busy looking at her worksheet, thinking about the last thing on the list: *depression*.

If being really, really sad was genetic, wouldn't that mean being really angry sometimes was, too?

If Joey was going to figure any of this out, she was going to have to find their donor.

After school, Joey put her gym clothes on for the first time in weeks as Mom drove Joey, Colton, and Layla to the Red Bank Armory ice rink. They kind of smelled (had she washed them since the last time she wore them?) but they were good enough. It was the first day of hockey practice, and tryouts for the team were at the end of the week.

Thomas was a baseball player, so he didn't want to play. Colton, on the other hand, didn't have the patience for baseball—he'd stand in the outfield and make shadow puppets on the grass—and had quit Little League two years ago. Joey never wanted to try softball in the first place.

She was never really interested in sports. She wasn't entirely sure she was interested in them now, but she wanted to make Benny happy, and when she asked Mom if she could try out, Mom just got so freaking excited. "Yes! Yes, you absolutely can play! Oh my God, I love this. Do you want to watch a preseason game with me to get ready? I'm sure there will be one on TV . . ."

There wasn't one on TV, but that didn't stop Mom from talking about it all week. She lent Joey her Blackhawks sweatshirt again, to wear during practice, and Joey put it on, feeling warm from both the heavy fabric and the smile Mom had given her.

Mom honked the horn at the person in front of them, who hadn't moved the moment the light turned green. Mom was fairly impatient about that, which drove Mama nuts. Joey glanced over at Layla, in the seat next to her. Layla wasn't trying out for the team or anything. She just wanted to tag along, and Mom said yes before Joey could express her opinion.

Joey was the only girl at practice, which she was anticipating. Luka said she could play, but still she found herself sitting alone on the bench as she attempted to tie up her skates, while all the boys were loud and chatty and huddled together as they put on their skates and ran out onto the ice. Joey watched as Colton nearly slipped and nose-dived upon entry.

Layla was up in the stands with Mom, watching. Joey tried really hard to forget that Layla was there. She didn't need the distraction.

Luka blew his whistle. "Alright, everyone! Let's see what you got!"

The older Benny got, the more Joey realized he sounded just like his dad. She could hear Benny's voice in Luka's, and it put her a little at ease.

Joey's feet were wobbly in her skates; she didn't

think they were tied tightly enough. Benny had showed her years ago how to wrap the laces around her ankles to keep them extra sturdy, but she didn't think she'd done it right.

Joey sighed, making her way to the ice. She could do this.

The only problem was, Joey realized pretty quickly that she was absolutely no good at hockey.

Colton wasn't great at it, either, but at least the rest of the boys gave Colton a chance. They'd pass him the puck. They'd cheer him on. They'd actually let him play. When Joey was wide open, right in front of the net with a clear shot because Jackson was way too small and terrible to be goalie, Eli completely ignored her. Then Isaac took the puck from him and sped off to the other end.

"What was that about?" Joey yelled, the words coming out muffled through her mouthguard. "I was wide open, Eli."

He continued to ignore her, so Joey grabbed his shirtsleeve and tugged.

"Get off of me," Eli said, shaking free. "No one even wants to play with you, Joey."

"I haven't done anything."

"Yeah? Tell that to Danny's collarbone, Bruiser," Eli said, skating away.

Joey slowed to a stop and glanced up at the bleachers. Mom was there, big smile on her face, sitting next to Layla. It made Joey's chest feel tight and her shoulders tense. They were up there, watching her, and she wanted to impress them.

She *needed* to impress them.

But she couldn't do that if no one would let her play, so if they weren't going to pass her the puck, she'd have to get it herself. Good thing Benny had taught her to skate years ago; she was, at least, faster than most of the boys on the ice. She might be a little off balance with the hockey stick, and she couldn't really hit the puck with as much strength as she needed because of it, but this she could do.

She picked up speed, ignoring the way her ankles hurt (she definitely hadn't tied her skates enough), and found herself shoulder to shoulder with Eli. She nudged him a bit, making her almost lose her footing.

"Stop," he said. "We're on the same side."

"Give me the puck," she said. She used her stick to

try and take it from him, but she really wasn't all that graceful, slapping it on the ice around the puck and never quite touching it.

"Joey, *stop*."

"You're being a ball hog!"

"It's a *puck*, Joey!" Only, this time he didn't say Joey. He used the *B* word that had been banned from Joey's household back a couple years ago when Benny used it to refer the girl who just broke up with him. Joey had never seen Mama so mad at Benny, and she'd lectured Colton and Thomas while she was at it.

Eli laughed to himself after he said it, as if it were the funniest thing in the world.

So Joey used the hook of her stick to pull at Eli's leg, knocking him off balance and sending him spiraling on the ice, the puck free for the taking.

The only good thing was that roughhousing happened *plenty* during hockey, so Mom spared Joey the lecture and Luka sent Joey home with a rule book, since tripping was apparently not allowed. Eli had complained about a girl trying out for the team for the rest of the practice, saying she had to resort to cheating to keep up, but he was *fine*. A bunch of them fell during practice anyway.

Joey was sore, though, as she and her brothers helped Mom go through their things in storage. So was Colton, who kept pawning off the bigger boxes on Thomas as the three of them went through their belongings. Their moms had found a house to rent, and Mama was determined not to move all of their old junk into the new place. She thought they could use a nice "cleanse," so while she finished up her work for the day at the motel, Joey, the boys, and Mom had the job of deciding what exactly needed cleansing from their stuff in storage.

Joey's legs burned a little as she squatted down to pick up a box, moving it to the side to look at what was under it. Everything was covered in dust, which Joey thought was ridiculous. It hadn't been *that* long. "This one has baby clothes," she said.

"Oh! Let me see," Mom said, practically cooing. "I can't believe you guys ever fit into any of this. You were so teeny!"

"That's because the boys took up too much space for us to grow in Mama's womb," Joey said.

"Ew," Colton said. "Don't talk about Mama's *womb*."

Mom threw a pale pink onesie at his head. "Your mother's womb, just like everything about her, is beautiful."

"Why doesn't Benny have to help?" Colton asked. "Some of this stuff is his, you know."

Mom sighed. "Yes, I do know. But Benny is spending some time with his dad, and he'll be around to help once we move into the new place, that I promise you."

"So he's moving in with us, right?" Joey asked.

Mom's smile was tight. "Of course, sweets. It'll all go back to normal."

"This box just has a bunch of folders and papers," Thomas said.

Mom motioned for him to bring it over to her. "That's probably all our important documents. Birth certificates and stuff. Mama was mad I didn't bring it to the motel, but I thought it was safer here."

"Birth certificates?" Joey asked. She stood up, ignoring the soreness in her ankles (hockey was *rough*, okay?) and bent to peek into the box. She bit the inside of her cheek, hard, before asking, "Is there . . . I mean, does the box have papers about the donor, too?"

Mom paused, papers in her hands, her eyes still in the box. "Probably, yeah," she answered slowly. "Why?"

Joey shrugged a shoulder, trying not to look all that interested. "What sorts of things do you know about him? Do the papers say anything about him? Like, what he's like, or whatever?"

Mom didn't answer right away. She put the papers back into the box and closed it. "It was an anonymous donor. We know his medical history. That's about it."

"Can I see it?" Joey asked.

Thomas was looking at her funny, his eyebrows pinched and his mouth tight. Colton seemed to be ignoring the conversation altogether, digging deep into one of the boxes.

"Um," Mom cleared her throat. "Sure, babe. But, you know, let's just get this box home, yeah? We'll look through it there, so we don't lose track of anything here. Okay? I'm going to go bring this to the car quick."

Joey nodded, and Mom picked up the box and left the boys and Joey in the storage room. Joey had pushed aside the box of baby clothes to open another when she realized her brothers were looking at her. "What?"

"You just hurt her feelings," Thomas said.

"What?" Joey raised her eyebrows. "How?"

"Why'd you ask about the donor anyway?" Colton asked. "It's weird to think about. And kind of gross? I don't think I want to think about *that*."

Joey clenched her jaw, feeling defensive. "Aren't you ever curious? It's important to know where you come from. Like Layla and her mom, with their ancestry thing. And all that stuff in Mr. Hoover's class."

"I don't know," Colton said. "It's just all too weird. It's not like I wanna know the guy. We have Luka, and Benny. And moms, obviously."

"I still think you hurt her feelings," Thomas said.

Joey shook her head. "I'm not even asking because of Mom. It has nothing to do with her."

Thomas pulled open another box. It was full of Christmas ornaments. "Maybe at least just go talk to her?" He handed Joey the box of Christmas ornaments. "Here, you should take these to her and tell her you're sorry."

"But I'm *not* sorry," Joey snapped at him. She wasn't. She hadn't done anything wrong. She just wanted to know if that feeling in her stomach, the one that pressed down on her lungs and made her want to scream and fight . . . if the donor felt that way, too. If that was part of *him*, like it was part of Joey.

She looked over at Colton for support, but he said, "Just go, okay?"

Joey sighed. "Fine."

~~~~~•

Mom was behind the car, trunk open, half inside and half out as she moved things around to fit. She stood up straight, observing the inside of the trunk as the wind whipped her hair around. Joey couldn't help but compare it to Mama's hair in the breeze on top of the hill at Hartshorne Park. Mom's hair, straighter and lighter, looked almost like sunrays surrounding her head.

Joey walked up behind her with the box in her hand. "Um. Christmas ornaments," she said.

Mom reached for the box and put it in the trunk with the rest of them.

"Um." Joey took a breath. "I only asked because we're doing genetics in our science unit. About the donor, I mean."

"It's totally fine, my love. You don't need to explain." Mom winked at Joey, before quickly looking away and

68

focusing back on the boxes in the car. They fit fine, but Mom was shifting them around again anyway.

Mom did that, though. She made sure things fit. In their old apartment, she moved beds and furniture over and over again, every time one of the triplets needed space—when Thomas wanted a new bookcase, when Joey needed her own closet. Even when Colton had begged for his own room, Mom had tried to make the walk-in pantry work. It didn't. Colton said it reminded him a little too much of a coffin, but she'd tried. If Joey and her brothers decided that every box in that storage room needed to come home, Mom would shift everything in their car so that they could.

Mom stood back, hands on her hips, admiring her work. She had a crooked smile on her face, the one she sometimes got when she was proud of Colton for actually doing well on a test, or when Benny had played a particularly good hockey game. Joey suddenly thought about Mom in the bleachers at the end of *her* hockey practice, wearing that same smile. It was her *I'm proud,* smile, and Joey started thinking about that, about that crooked proud smile on Mom's face and the way she'd bump her shoulder into Layla's every time Colton or Joey did something on the ice.

Which shifted Joey's thoughts to Layla. Which wasn't supposed to happen.

"I don't want you to think . . . it's okay to be curious, Little Growl," Mom said. "We'll talk about it more with Mama later, okay?"

"When did you know you were in love with Mama?"

The question startled Mom, who pulled her head out of the trunk to focus on Joey. It startled Joey, too. She didn't even mean to ask it.

"Shortly after we met," Mom said, her voice as soft as it always was when she talked about Mama. "She was such a kind, sweet little dweeb. How could I not fall for her?"

It made Joey smile, even if it wasn't the answer she wanted. "No. I mean, how did you know . . . that you liked Mama . . . even though she was a girl?"

"Oh," Mom said. She sat down on the back of the car, patting the spot next to her for Joey to join her. "Well. That's a different conversation all together. I always . . . knew I felt different. I just, didn't really know? Or at least, I didn't want to think about it, because I was confused for a long time. I married Luka, because I thought that's what I wanted. I don't regret it, because I love your brother Benny and wouldn't trade him for the world. But something was missing, with Luka. With me. When I met your mama, I found that something."

"Did it ever scare you?" Joey asked. "Knowing that she was that something?"

Mom's smile seemed sad. "Terrified me. But you never need to know that fear, if you ever feel that way. You know that, right? I never want you to feel like I did. Mama and I only want you all to be happy, no matter what. No matter who you love."

Joey looked away. "Are you ever afraid you'll hurt her?"

"All the time, every day," Mom said.

It was the first time she said anything in a long while that Joey completely understood.

That night, under the covers so that no one would see the glow from her cell phone, Joey scrolled through her contacts for Layla's name.

Joey couldn't stop thinking about Layla sitting in the bleachers, couldn't stop thinking about the box of important documents that Mom still had in the trunk of her car. Mom didn't talk to Mama about it, like she said she would. Mom spent all of dinner recapping for Mama every single thing Joey and Colton had done during hockey practice, talking animatedly with her hands in a way that made rice fling off her fork. She kept bumping her shoulder against Joey's, trying to get her to laugh.

Joey couldn't bring up the donor during that.

She'd try again tomorrow. She wasn't even sure if it would help her much. She still couldn't wait to get her hands on that paperwork, but it didn't sound good that the donor was anonymous. That complicated things. Joey googled *anonymous donors* and discovered that what her moms *did* know about him wouldn't actually be all that much. Basically just his physical attributes and whether or not he was healthy.

Joey had to assume the paperwork said he *was* healthy. Her moms wouldn't pick a donor if his medical form said something like "Might yell or punch or get mad for no reason." Whatever was on that paper wouldn't be enough to tell Joey anything.

Layla and her mom had spent *hours* tracing their lineage. She knew exactly how to find relatives based on their shared DNA. She'd been doing it all year. She kept an entire notebook about it; she and her mom had this family-tree map hung up in her bedroom.

If anyone would be able to dig up actual information about a donor Joey knew nothing about, it would be Layla.

Joey sent Layla a text for the first time in what felt like forever:

Hi. I need your help with something

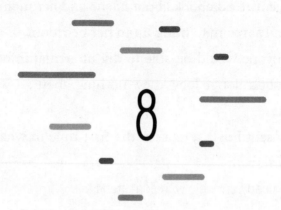

8

The hardest part of setting her plan in motion
wasn't the fact that Layla was clearly mad at Joey (even
though, yes, that was a problem, too)—it was that
Colton was *everywhere* Layla was, during school.

Which meant Joey had to talk to Layla alone in the
girls' bathroom. She couldn't let Colton know about
this.

Colton probably wouldn't even *want* to know about
this, so really, Joey was doing him a favor.

That was what she told herself, anyway.

Joey was leaning against the sink when Layla
walked in.

"Okay," Layla said, crossing her arms over her chest. "What do you want?"

The right way to begin this conversation, Joey knew, would be to apologize to Layla so that Layla might actually be willing to help her. But the words were stuck somewhere in Joey's throat. She couldn't say them. Sometimes apologizing felt like admitting there was something wrong with her. Even if she really was sorry.

"I need your help looking for something," Joey said in place of an apology. "You'd have to invite me over. We could do it on your computer."

"Wait a second. So, you ignore me and don't want to hang out with me until you need me for something?" Layla said, tugging on one of her hoodie strings. "That's not cool, Joey. Why should I even help you?"

She probably shouldn't. Joey had done everything she could, on purpose, to get Layla to stop calling her *friend*. Mama had even asked about it, but Joey had shrugged her off.

"I don't know what else to do," Joey said, because it was true. And if Layla could help her . . . maybe she wouldn't have to keep pushing Layla away. Maybe this could not only help Joey keep Mom and Benny, but Layla, too. "I just really need your help, Layla."

Layla huffed, but her expression softened. She unfolded her arms. "Fine. But the minute you get nasty or yell at me or something, Joey, I'm not helping you anymore. Deal?"

"Deal," Joey agreed quickly. "So . . . can I come over after school, or what?"

~•~•~•~•

It had been a while since Joey was in Layla's house. Being in Layla's room again, with her bright green comforter still the same, her ridiculous collection of stuffed pigs still lined up against her pillows in the exact same order they were always in, made Joey pause in the doorway. Layla had clothes on the floor *near* her hamper, not in it, just like she always did, and her books were stacked on the floor next to her bed instead of in the bookcase across the room.

It was all like Joey had expected it to be, and she couldn't explain why that made her throat suddenly feel tight.

Layla was sitting at her computer desk, tugging on one of the strings of her hoodie again, leaving one much, much longer than the other. Joey wanted to reach for those strings and make them even again. She ignored that impulse. She couldn't touch Layla's hoodie. She couldn't get too close to Layla at all.

So Joey sat awkwardly across the room on Layla's bed, even though she used to always sit right below Layla's desk on the floor. The last time she was here, in Layla's room, sitting on the floor next to Layla's desk chair, she had tickled the bottom of Layla's sock-clad foot. Layla almost kicked her.

Joey didn't want to think about the rest of it.

"Your, uh, tree. It's getting bigger," Joey said, motioning toward Layla's family-tree map on her wall. There were way more branches and dates, going back further than the last time Joey was here. It nearly took up the entire wall.

"So what do you need my help with?" Layla asked. "And why couldn't Colton come, too? He's super annoyed, by the way. I don't think he believed me when I said you were coming over."

"I'll deal with Colton later." Joey waved it off. He'd texted her like fifteen times already. Mostly just a bunch of question marks.

Joey reached into her pocket for the copy of the

anonymous donor form Mama had finally given her. Her moms believed it was for school. Joey hadn't corrected them. "If you want to talk about this more with us, whenever you want, we certainly can," Mama had said. Mom didn't say much of anything, but neither did Joey. She just nodded with a closed-lip smile and took the paper.

"I need to find out who this guy is," Joey explained now to Layla. "I have some things I need to know about him."

Layla took the paper, before looking wide-eyed back at Joey. "You want to find your dad?"

"No, that's *not* what I said," Joey snapped, grabbing the paper roughly back from Layla.

"Hey!" Layla shouted back. "I said you can't get mad at me or I won't help you!"

"Okay! Okay, I didn't mean to," Joey said. "But he's *not* my dad, he's just a donor, and I don't want to find him, not really. This isn't about, like, wanting to meet him or anything like that."

"Then what *is* it about?" Layla asked.

Joey took a really, really deep breath. "I know that the other kids at school don't want anything to do with me. I know I was, like, the only one not invited to Aubrey's party, and that no one ever texts me to hang out because I'm . . ."

"Mean?" Layla said.

Joey felt her face flush hot. The way Layla said it, easily, as if it was the obvious answer, made Joey's stomach hurt. "I'm not . . . I mean, I can't . . ." She didn't know how to explain, and she felt that feeling again, the one that sat hard on her chest. The one that stayed right there, pressing down hard, unless she started screaming. "I don't mean to be."

Layla nodded. "I know that, Joey. I *know* you. You stopped talking to *me*, remember? Not the other way around."

"I know," Joey said. She didn't want to talk about that, though. Not right now. Not with Layla sitting so close to her after so long. Not after trying so, so hard to make those feelings go away.

"What does all that have to do with this, though?" Layla asked.

"I need to know if he ever felt like I do," Joey said. "Because if it's genetic, then it'll all make sense, you know? And I can prove to my mom that I'm not . . .

Look, I just really need you to do this for me. Please, Layla." She glanced up at the family-tree map. At all of the relatives Layla and her mom had discovered. "Find him for me?"

Layla's gaze moved to look up at the tree, too. She nodded. "Leave me the donor form. I'll see what I can do."

The day before they were going to move into their newly rented house, Mama wanted to take Joey for another hike on the Hartshorne Park trails. It was chilly enough now that they needed jackets. Joey didn't exactly know why they were doing this. It wasn't like Mama was dragging the boys out for after-school strolls.

"Come on, Jo-Jo! Keep up!" Mama called back. She was basically speed-walking. Joey didn't feel like running to catch up. "You need to stay in shape for hockey anyway, don't you?"

"I'm not out of shape," Joey said.

"Prove it!"

Afterward, Joey was sweaty and dirty and barely had time to wash up. The new house was going to have two bathrooms, thank God. Joey was getting sick and tired of fighting five people for one shower. "You smell a bit, Growl," Mom said in the car.

"Mama hogged the shower when we got back," Joey grumbled.

Mama's face scrunched all up, looking concerned and appropriately guilty. "You should have knocked! I didn't realize the time, I'd have gotten out!"

Luka was having them all over for dinner, since most of their stuff from the hotel was all boxed up for the move in the morning. Besides two entire bathrooms, their new home had four bedrooms: one for their moms, one for Joey, and one that Colton and Thomas would share. And one for Benny, if he wanted it.

Joey wasn't entirely sure that he did. "If Benny decides he's staying at Luka's, can I have his room in the new house?" Colton had asked earlier that day.

"Absolutely not," Mom replied.

"Well, can't I ask him at least?"

"No, Colton. And you will leave it at that," Mom snapped. It almost made Joey feel good, to have someone else snapping for once. And not even at her.

Even if the thought of an empty bedroom that belonged to Benny made her stomach ache.

"I'll almost miss having to be all snuggled up and

close in this motel," Mama had said, pulling Thomas in close for emphasis.

Joey absolutely did not agree. "I'm definitely looking forward to having space."

That night after dinner, she was once again enjoying the space at Luka's place, sprawled out on his living room couch while the parents finished cleaning in the kitchen. Benny was on the sofa across the room, studying for a test he had the next day. Thomas was sitting on the other end of the couch, and his leg kept bumping into Joey. She kicked it off her.

He still was touching her. She kicked him harder. "Joey, stop. There's no *room*," Thomas said.

If he wasn't sitting with his legs pulled up and crossed underneath him, if he was sitting straight on the couch like a normal person, there would be plenty of room. Every time his knee brushed against her, Joey felt herself tense even more. She reached over and pushed at him. "*Move*, Thomas!"

"Stop, guys. I need to finish reading this," Benny said.

Thomas bumped her back with his leg. "*You* move. You don't own the entire couch."

"Stop fighting," Colton said from his spot on the floor in front of the TV.

"Tell that to Joey!" Thomas said, then turned to Joey to say, "You think you're the only person in this family but you're actually the *worst* person in this family!"

Joey bit down on her tongue and kicked her leg into Thomas as hard as she could from where she was sitting.

Thomas yelled. "Ow! That hurt! What is *wrong* with you! I *hate* you!"

"Shut up, Thomas!" Joey shouted back.

"Jesus, are you serious, Joey?" Benny yelled. "Mom! Do something about this? This is exactly what I've been talking about."

Joey didn't like the sound of that. "*What* have you been talking about?"

"Hey!" Mom poked her head into the living room. "What on earth is going on in here?"

"I can't study with all of this," Benny said. "It's been so much easier since I've been here."

"Okay, you know what, Benny, I don't want to hear it. You're moving in with us tomorrow, end of conversation." Mom said. "Joey, come help us finish cleaning the dishes. Sounds like you all need some separation out here."

Joey pushed off of the couch and stormed into the kitchen. Luka was putting things away, and Mama was at the sink.

"Go dry the dishes for Mama," Mom said, gently pushing Joey in that direction. "You need to stop taunting Thomas. It's not right, and you know better."

"He wouldn't move!"

"I don't want to hear it, Joey, go help your mama."

Joey took a spot next to Mama, who handed her a dish. Joey picked up the towel and started drying it.

Her mom picked up the bottle of wine and refilled her and Luka's glasses. "See what I mean?" she said, handing Luka his glass before making her way over to the leftovers, covering them in foil to put them away. "And you think Becca and me should have more kids. Ridiculous, Luka!"

Luka laughed. "I was just asking! You wanted more, I remember you had a whole plan! And with Benny staying here instead—"

"First of all, Benny is moving into the new place with us. He'll be just fine once he realizes he still has his own room and privacy. Secondly, that baby plan changed the moment we found out we were having three at once," Mom said. "Our plan was for two. We got that and a bonus without having to wait."

"You're the one who always said you wanted to get pregnant again," Luka said. "Wasn't that what you two were gonna do? Becca carries and gives birth to the first, and then Steph, you were gonna carry using one of your eggs, or whatever?"

Joey froze, dried dish in her hands. She didn't know that.

"Please do *not* talk about my eggs," Mom said, cringing.

Mama suddenly pulled the dried dish out of Joey's hands. "Let's change the subject, huh?" she said to Mom and Luka. "When there aren't little ears helping me dry dishes, maybe."

Mom reached over to squeeze Joey's arm. Joey flinched; she didn't think Mom noticed. "I doubt Joey wants another sibling running around, anyway. We got more than what we bargained for," Mom said with a wink. "Besides, I did it already, I had one of my own. I think we're pretty set now."

Joey wondered what Mom's baby would look like.

A little boy with blond hair who told corny jokes and had their mom's smile. A little girl with blue eyes who was great at hockey like Benny. A nice little kid who made friends easily and never hit or broke things or screamed at the top of their lungs.

One of my own, Mom had said.

Joey had to find a way, and fast, to make sure Mom always considered Joey one of her own, too.

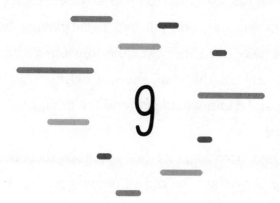

9

Mom was sitting in the bleachers again. She was by herself, wearing her favorite Blackhawks beanie, gloves on her hands, watching them practice.

It was the end of practice, and Luka was splitting them up to scrimmage three-on-three. Decisions would be made about who was on the team this weekend, and this was basically their last chance to prove themselves. Colton had actually scored a goal earlier, and Mom went nuts. Colton had pulled his helmet off and yelled at her to keep it down.

Joey wanted to have a reason to make Mom cheer so loud she'd have to tell her to keep it down.

Joey wasn't thrilled she was saddled with Colton

and Eli on her team. Colton had way better stick control than she did, and Eli had been playing hockey since he was five. She was quite obviously the third sucky wheel. At this rate, she was definitely going to get cut, and Mom would get to watch it happen.

Great.

Eli had been singling her out since the very first practice. Any time she did something wrong, he was the first to point it out. "There's no women's hockey league for a reason, Bruiser," he kept telling her.

Which wasn't even true. Mom had told Joey all about it a couple nights ago during a rare moment where they sat around, just the two of them. The NJ Devils were on TV, and Mom was only half watching as she sat with her laptop appropriately in her lap while she scrolled through their online bills. Joey was only in the room with her because Mom had called for one of them, and Joey was the closest in earshot. She was still getting used to that—the space of a new house where they had to actually call for one another instead of being right next to each other in a crowded motel room.

Someone had knocked their data over the limit this month, so the cell phone bill was higher than usual. Mom wanted Joey to show her how to find the page to see who the culprit was. "Ugh, it's Mama. Probably from the crappy motel wi-fi going in and out while she was trying to work." Mom groaned.

Joey bit back the snarky response that Mom shouldn't have assumed it was one of the triplets.

That was when the Devils scored, and Mom pulled her reading glasses off to watch the replay. "Hey, come here. Watch this with me," she said, and when Joey sat on the couch, Mom wrapped an arm around her.

They watched in silence for a bit, but it felt nice. Mom's arm was warm around Joey. The walls of the living room were still bare—Mama was still unpacking and decorating since they'd moved in—and it was always weird getting used to someplace new. But Joey liked this. She liked that her brothers were somewhere upstairs, and she was alone here with Mom.

A fight broke out between two of the hockey players, and the crowd was going wild. Joey braced herself for a lecture, her shoulders tensing, waiting for Mom to make sure Joey knew there would absolutely be *no* fighting, *or else*.

But Mom started laughing. "I don't think Luka would be too pleased if one broke out during your games, but God, I love a good hockey fight."

Joey shot her a skeptical look. "Really?"

"Really! But don't tell Mama." Mom winked. Two more players joined in the fight, and they started pulling them all apart to send them to the penalty box. "So much testosterone."

Well, that was true both on TV and on Joey's actual team. "I wish girls played hockey."

Mom bumped her shoulder against Joey's. "You think you're the only one? There's a women's national hockey team! They win gold or silver in, like, every tournament they play. They don't televise any women's sports like they should, and don't get me started on that. But I'll figure out how we can watch a women's game together. I promise. Okay?"

She smiled, big and crooked, and Joey smiled, too. "Okay."

Not that knowing about the women's team helped Joey much now. Eli didn't seem to care much about the actual truth about women's hockey.

The scrimmage started, and of course, Eli had the puck first. Joey doubted he would pass it to Colton, let alone her. He was a ball hog in gym class and a puck hog here.

Joey tried really hard to focus on the sound of skates

on ice, on the other kids shouting from the sidelines, and not on Mom. Mom was supposed to be quiet— Luka told her she had to be if she insisted on coming to watch—but she was cheering like wild anyway. She had spent the entire drive here giving Joey and Colton pointers, and Joey had eagerly listened to her, while Colton stared bored out the car window. Mom had noticed. She patted Joey on the thigh with a wink and said, "I'm so glad you're liking this."

Joey snuck a glance up at the bleachers. Mom gave her a big thumbs-up.

Before practice, all morning, Mom had been pretty quiet. She'd actually been kind of quiet since the night before, so it was a nice change seeing her look so happy now. Benny had technically moved in with them to the new place, but he was officially splitting his time between houses more than he used to. He stayed at Luka's last night, even though he was supposed to spend the night home with them. "I told Dad I'd watch the game with him, and I have a huge test tomorrow. I need peace and quiet to study for it," Benny had said.

Mom had mumbled under her breath, "I wish I had somewhere to leave and have peace and quiet some-times, too." Which made Mama wrap an arm around

Mom and tell her to stop pouting and it all made Joey wonder if Mom really meant it.

Mom cheered loudly in the bleachers again, pulling Joey from her thoughts.

Eli was blocked by two of the other kids they were scrimmaging against, and he passed to Colton, who couldn't get anywhere, either. Colton passed back to Eli, which annoyed Joey, because she was open, too, and them playing back-and-forth wasn't going to do anything. (She maybe wasn't the best at passing the puck, but they could still let her try.)

They passed it back and forth *again*, and Joey sighed. Eli definitely wasn't going to let her be a part of this, and Colton didn't have good access to her. Joey figured she might as well try and clear a path for one of them so they could at least do *something*.

Eli was backed against the wall by Jackson, and Joey quickly skated over, throwing her shoulder into Jackson, checking him against that wall and clearing the way for Eli to skate off.

It got louder in the rink, shouts from the other boys echoing around the room, as Eli got up close to the net and shot the puck.

It went in. Luka blew his whistle—the scrimmage was over, and Joey's team won.

"Yes!" Colton yelled, skating over to Joey and bopping her on the helmet. "Awesome block!"

Eli came up and held out his fist for Joey to bump, too. "Nicely done, Bruiser," he said. "Guess you're useful after all."

It wasn't a great compliment, but Joey would take it anyway.

"Great work, Joey. We still need to work on your stick work, but defense might just be the way to go," Luka said as Joey skated off the ice. She tried not to smile but couldn't help it. She'd done something good.

Joey looked up at the bleachers and saw her mom standing, clapping her hands and pointing at Joey with a big smile on her face.

10

The hockey boys all started calling Joey "Bruiser," even at school. (Danny Carter, whose collarbone wasn't exactly totally healed yet, hadn't seemed thrilled when he heard it, though.) In gym class that week, they even tried getting Luka to let her participate again.

"Can't Joey be on my team?" Colton said, and some of the boys nodded their heads in hopeful agreement.

"She's got two weeks left to go before I can let her back," Luka said. "Consequences are consequences regardless of how decent she might be at hockey."

Eli laughed. *"Decent."*

Still, it was a nice change from the hockey team not

wanting to play with her at all. Even so, Joey didn't mind that Luka held his ground. She sat up in the bleachers watching the class play a game of speedball, pretending to do her homework as usual. Every so often, Luka would catch her watching and not working, and motion for her to get busy. She kept her pencil in her hand and her math notebook in her lap, so it looked like she was doing something other than doodling.

"Hey!" Layla's voice was suddenly in her ear, and Joey turned to realize just how close Layla was sitting to her. The hair that wasn't tucked into the back of Layla's hoodie brushed against Joey's shoulder. "How's the new home? I gotta come over and see it."

Joey blushed, and scooted over to give them both a little more room. "It's better than the motel. Forget your gym clothes again?"

"More like forgot to wash them," Layla said. "Since my choice was to wear them and have that smell on me all day or sit out for the day, I chose the lesser of two evils and told Coach Cooper I left them home. Besides, I wanted to talk to you."

Joey's stomach felt a little like she'd eaten rocks. She tried to smile, but it felt a little wobbly. "What about?"

"Your donor."

"Oh," Joey said, and those rocks tumbled around in her stomach. Of course that was what Layla wanted. Joey rolled her shoulders and nodded her head. "Okay. Did you find something? Were you able to do anything?"

Layla gave a sheepish smile. "Not exactly? They have a ton of resources out there for kids of donors, did you know that? But if you went that route, you'd either have to be eighteen or have your moms deal with all of this. Which . . . since you decided to start talking to *me*, I'm guessing that's no good."

Joey shook her head, shoulders slumping. "No. I kind of just wanted you to do the whole ancestry detective thing for me yourself."

Layla hesitated. "Are you sure? Because your moms seem like they'd be okay with helping you with this. If you asked them."

"I don't want my moms to know about this."

"I figured," Layla said. "And I did play around, but, well . . . I'm gonna need a bit more from you."

Layla moved even closer to Joey, thigh to thigh, and slipped her cell phone out of her hoodie pocket and put it on top of Joey's notebook. She put her hand on top of Joey's, where Joey was holding the notebook, and positioned the notebook so that Luka couldn't see the cell phone behind it. Joey swallowed, but it went down her throat hard. Layla smelled like her favorite vanilla lotion that she used for the dry skin on her elbows and knees, and it made Joey kind of dizzy up close.

Layla quickly typed on her phone, glancing up at Luka every few seconds to make sure he wasn't going to catch them. "So, the website my mom and I use is called 23andMe."

"Yeah, I know. You guys sent your saliva or whatever, right?" Joey said. Mama always freaked out when those commercials came on TV. Almost every time it would air, she'd comment, "The government is going to keep all our DNA on file to use however they want."

Layla scrolled through the website. "It connects you with people who are a match, genetically. I actually found a whole article about kids of donors using it to try and find their donor siblings and stuff when their donor was anonymous. It was wild. Something like thirty donor siblings met because of it."

Joey's throat got dry. She cleared it. She never really thought about other kids from the same donor. It made her a little uncomfortable. "I don't want that. Like, to know if there are other kids. They aren't really my brothers or sisters or anything, it's not like when you find your relatives. It's . . . different. I just want to know about, you know . . . the *source*."

"We can still use this to see if we can find him, then. It might not work, but it could. Mom and I have found *so* many people connected to us," Layla said. "We really just need to find out who he is, or some-one connected to him, even, that I can use to trace to him. I just need a starting point. But the thing is, Joey, I can't do it without, well, you signing up and starting it."

Joey wasn't sure about that. "Oh. I don't know. Doesn't it cost a ton of money?"

Layla nodded. "Yeah. Basic level is about a hundred. I have some money saved? I always keep the change when my dad gives me money for the movies and stuff. And you have a birthday soon, you always get money from your grandparents at least. I can tell my mom I've been saving money and want to buy something on Etsy, or whatever, and she'll put it in her account and let me use the PayPal. Oh! It also says something about if you're female that it's best to test a male in the family, too, for some reason? But I'm sure I can get Colton to give me a swab, no worries. I'll figure something out, he won't say no to me."

Joey looked away. She didn't like to think about all the time Layla and Colton spent together without her, especially lately.

"I know this is . . . a lot," Layla said, misunderstanding Joey's hesitation. "Especially since, well, neither you *or* Colton ever talked about the donor before. If you change your mind, if you decide you don't want to . . . I won't do it. But it's been really cool tracing my roots with my mom. Maybe this could be really cool for you, too."

The bell rang; gym class was over. Layla quickly scooted her phone back into her pocket, standing. Joey looked up at her, missing the warmth of Layla's leg against hers. Layla was watching Joey expectantly, and yes, Joey had pushed Layla away for a reason, but still . . . she wanted *this* reason to keep talking to her. She wanted to find a way to fix things.

If she could figure this out, she wouldn't have to be afraid of hurting Layla.

Which meant she was going to have to really do this. "I'll try and get you the money."

Layla smiled. "Don't worry, Joey. I bet this'll be fun."

~◦~◦~◦~◦

This was what happened, four months ago, at the start of the summer: Joey realized she had more than "best friends" feelings for Layla. Nothing big happened. It wasn't like in the movies where someone sees the person across the room and there are fireworks and swelling music and grand gestures. It was actually no different from any other day.

All that happened was that they were sitting in Layla's room, with Layla on her desk chair and Joey right beside her, like they'd done *literally* a million times before. Joey reached up to tickle Layla's foot, which she'd never done, but Layla had on the socks that Joey gave her for her birthday, the ones with the funny little trees on them. Layla laughed, and Joey felt warm. When Layla looked down at her, Joey suddenly wondered what it would be like to kiss her.

It was a thought that Joey couldn't get out of her head for the rest of the night.

She also thought about the fact that Layla probably wouldn't like *her* that way, because Layla wasn't gay (was Joey gay?), and Joey's chest felt tight at the thought that things could get messed up now. That feeling made Joey angry. When Layla came over the next day to hang out with her and Colton, when Layla laughed with Colton, and sat close to Colton, that anger grew and grew and grew.

Layla had shoved herself on the couch between Colton and Joey. Joey pushed her off, and Layla shifted to sit more on Colton. Joey didn't like that either, so she shoved Layla as hard as she could onto the floor.

Layla hit her elbow on the coffee table in front of them.

She was okay; she got a small bruise and cried, but she didn't bleed or anything. Joey—after getting in trouble first from Colton and then her moms, who came rushing into the room to see what happened— shut herself into her bedroom and tried not to cry, too.

She stopped talking to Layla right after. Layla was probably mad, anyway, and Joey knew it was all her fault that she was feeling this way. Layla didn't like Joey like that. Joey needed to stop liking Layla that way, too.

That was what Joey was thinking about as Layla walked with her to science class. Colton had caught up with the both of them after changing out of his gym clothes, and he kept looking between the two of them as if he was searching for something.

"What?" Joey asked, when it got on her nerves.

Colton shrugged. "Nothing."

They took their seats in Mr. Hoover's class, and Mr. Hoover got them all settled quickly before passing out what Joey assumed were more worksheets. "Before we dive in today, I wanted to talk a bit about the projects you'll be doing to complete this unit."

Joey tried not to groan. She hated projects, mostly because they almost always had to do them in groups or pairs.

"You are all going to pair up for this," Hoover said, proving Joey right. "I'll let you choose your partners, but if there're any issues, I reserve the right to change my mind and pick them myself."

He handed Joey the project guidelines, and she looked at them. It said NATURE VS. NURTURE at the top in big letters.

"While studying nature versus nurture, scientists focus on specific study groups. They observe these groups, and their characteristics and behaviors, to then draw conclusions," Mr. Hoover said. "Which is exactly what you'll be doing. You and your partner will decide on a specific person or persons to study. You'll decide on your hypothesis: Is nature or nurture more prominent with your subject? Then you'll observe, take notes, and draw conclusions."

"That's it?" Colton asked.

Mr. Hoover laughed. "Well, you'll have a research paper to write together as well, plus you'll have to present to the class."

Joey raised her hand. "So you're saying we have to prove that genetics play the most important role in all this?"

"That's your hypothesis, Joey. I'm asking everyone to try and prove their own."

Layla raised her hand next. "Since we have an odd number in the class, can Colton, Joey, and I work together?"

That took Joey by surprise. It was something they had started doing in fourth grade, once Layla realized that odd numbers always meant *someone* got to work in threes. But now, when things were still so weird, Joey didn't know why Layla would want to.

Based on the way Colton's head moved back and forth between Joey and Layla, neither did he. "So you two *are* talking again?" Colton asked.

"We have a good working relationship." Layla winked, and Joey nearly melted. "Besides, let's be honest. Your family is, like, the perfect test subject for this kind of project, and I want an A."

"So you're saying we're your lab rats," Joey mumbled.

Layla laughed, leaning in so she could pull Colton and Joey close and wrap an arm around the both of them. "Maybe lab mice. Mice are much cuter."

Joey's cheeks burned hot.

She tried to ignore the way Colton was looking at her.

The week came and went, and Joey was sitting, squished between Colton and Thomas, in front of a large cake that read in icing: *Happy Birthday Jo, Col, and Tom!*

(No one ever called Colton or Thomas either of those nicknames, but Mom started writing too big and needed to shorten their names to make it all fit.)

There were fifteen candles on top of the cake.

Twelve, since the triplets were turning twelve, plus one extra for each of them. "It's for good luck," Mama said, "and so that each of you can have your own special wish."

Benny was there, too. Joey wanted to ask if he was staying for the night, for the week, for a while, now that they were settled in the new place . . . but she couldn't bring herself to, just in case the answer was no. Mom had been hovering really close to him all night, fingers reaching for his shirtsleeve, as if she was afraid, too, of letting go.

Mom reached again for Benny, moving him to stand behind the triplets so that she could take a photo. "I want all my babies in the picture!" she said. "Wait, wait, it's on selfie mode. God, do I really look like this?"

"Mom! Come on, I want to eat the cake!" Colton said.

"Mama, go get in the photo," Mom said, pushing Mama over, too.

"What about you?" Mama asked.

"Oh my God, give me the phone," Benny said, taking it from Mom and pulling her close. "I have the longest arms, I'll take a selfie of all of us."

Joey, as happy as she was that Benny was there and

that Mama remembered to make a cake with chocolate frosting, wanted this part to be over with. She was sweating a little, surrounded by her whole family. Squished right in the center.

"Three, two, one, and . . . okay," Benny said, and then handed the phone back to Mom. "Are we gonna sing now?"

"Do we need to sing?" Joey groaned. "Let's just eat the cake."

"No, no, no," Mama said, reaching down to wrap Joey in a tight hug, kissing her cheek. "I want to sing!"

"You know better than to ask Mama not to sing," Benny said, laughing.

So, they sang. An off-key, awkward "Happy Birthday" that had Joey rolling her eyes and Colton and Thomas laughing the entire time. When their moms and Benny finally stopped (they dragged out that last *you* as long as they possibly could), the triplets all leaned forward, inhaling deeply and then blowing the candles out in one shot.

Their moms and Benny applauded, and Colton said, "Can we just eat the cake now, please?" Joey wiggled her way out from between her brothers, ducking under the table to come out free on the other side.

Mama grabbed paper plates and forks and pulled the cake closer so she could start cutting pieces. Colton and Thomas pulled out the candles to lick the frosting off the bottoms. Joey moved away from the group to stand back by the kitchen counter instead, needing some air.

Mom came over to stand next to her. "You're the oldest, you know. You can claim the first piece."

"I'm the oldest by, like, thirty seconds," Joey said.

"Felt like you were the oldest for hours from where I was standing. They wiped you down, wrapped you up, and put you right into my arms, all slimy and purple," Mom told her. "It was like the world stopped. It was nothing but you and me in those thirty seconds."

Joey thought about that. She tried to picture her mom, younger, standing on the side of the hospital bed, coaching Mama through what she describes as "the happiest and scariest day of my life." Mom knew what it was like to have a baby; she had had Benny, after all. But she didn't know what it was like to play the other role, the one Luka had played for her. Joey wondered if it felt different. Joey wondered if holding her felt different for her mom than when the doctor had handed her

Benny, when she was sweaty and tired in the hospital bed instead of standing next to it.

She couldn't ask, though. It didn't seem right to.

"I loved you so much from the moment I held you, slime and everything, you know that?" Mom said, as if she was in Joey's head with her. "You had this little wrinkled-old-man face, and it was the most beautiful thing I've ever seen. My daughter."

Mom wrapped her arms around Joey to hug her tight. Joey closed her eyes for a moment, just one short moment, letting herself enjoy it.

"Oh, I almost forgot," Mom said, letting go of Joey and moving away to where her bag sat on the counter. "I've got cards from your grandparents!"

She handed Joey a card before walking over to give Colton and Thomas theirs. Joey looked at the envelope, her name written in her grandmother's spiraling cursive. She pressed her fingers against it. It was thicker than just a card, and Joey knew from past experiences that meant there was money inside.

Which reminded Joey of Layla. Of 23andMe.

She looked back up at her moms and brothers. Colton and Benny both had slices of cake the size of their heads, and Thomas was eating just the frosting off of his like he always did. Mama was cutting a piece for Mom, moving to hand it to her before pulling it away, teasing her. Mom gave Mama a kiss, and Mama gave her the cake. Mama turned to look at Joey, holding up a piece of her own. "Coming to join us?" Mama asked.

Joey tucked the birthday card into her sweatshirt pocket to open later.

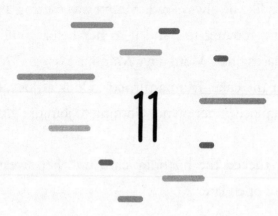

11

Joey and Thomas were fighting over what to watch on Netflix when Colton's cell phone buzzed with a text and Thomas's phone, which was sitting next to it on the coffee table, buzzed right after it.

They both reached for their phones. "Hey," Mom basically whined at them. "Can you stay off your phones for, like, twenty minutes or are you that codependent on them?"

Mom and Mama were lounging on the couch. Mom was lying across the cushions with Mama sitting between her legs.

Joey watched them exchange a look when Colton

said, "Eli is having a Halloween party Friday. Can we go?"

"It's a costume party," Thomas added.

"Halloween parties usually are," Joey said, taking the remote from him. She pulled her own phone out of her pocket. Hers had been on silent.

"Don't be such a jerk, Joey. It's not my fault if you weren't invited to this party either," Thomas said.

"Hey," Mom said. "Don't, Thomas."

Joey was surprised, though, because she actually had a text, too: Bruiser! Party at my house friday for halloween

It was the first party she had been invited to all year. "Actually," Joey said, holding up her phone so everyone could see it, "Eli wants me to come, too."

Mama reached out and Joey handed her the phone. Her moms exchanged another glance with each other. It made Joey want to reach over and yank her phone back.

Mama frowned at the screen. "*Bruiser*? Do I know Eli? Why is he calling you that?"

"It's just a nickname," Joey said. "Eli's on the hockey team with us."

"They all call Joey 'Bruiser,'" Colton said.

Mama scrunched up her nose. "Should I like that? I'm not sure if I like that."

"You'll get it once you see our kid on the ice! She's a natural!" Mom said with a wink that made Joey blush.

Mama groaned. "I can barely handle watching Benny play! It's so stressful, watching our baby get hit!"

"Don't worry," Colton said. "Bruiser over here is the one doing the hitting."

Mama groaned again, but Mom patted her leg. "It's good hitting, babe. A good outlet, just like Benny and Luka said. Like I was telling you! It's clearly good for her, the team's inviting her to this Halloween party." She smiled at Joey as if Joey had actually done something worth praising. It was an invite to Eli's stupid party, not an award of some sort.

"So we can go?" Colton asked. "To the party?"

"Yes. You can all go to the party."

~~~~~•

They picked up Layla on the way. She was dressed as Black Widow, and Joey had to look down at her feet when she felt the heat in her cheeks. Layla looked really,

really good in black leather, and Joey kind of felt super weird for thinking it (even though it was true).

Colton was dressed as Hawkeye (which Joey wasn't thrilled about; it made him and Layla a pair, even though they were all supposed to be together). Thomas was Captain America. Joey was Captain Marvel.

They weren't even huge superhero fans or anything. Joey had seen maybe, like, two of the movies. But they needed costumes quickly, and when Mom went to the Halloween store after work, she just grabbed what was easiest.

Mama drove them to Eli's house and parked out front. "Be polite to Eli's parents and call me if you need me," she said. "Mom's working late, but I'll be around all night."

Mama wanted to get out and walk them to the door, but all of them, Layla included, protested all at once, and loudly, and convinced her otherwise.

The second they walked through Eli's door, Joey found herself getting slammed against the wall, hard, with a loud *oof!*

"Got you, Bruiser!" Eli said, laughing maniacally in full hockey gear, in a jersey for the Mighty Ducks, whoever they were.

"Jesus, Eli!" Layla said. "Joey, are you okay?"

It hurt, but she sure as heck wasn't going to admit that in front of Layla *or* Eli. She shoved Eli, and then backhanded him against his helmet. "Get off of me, loser."

Eli shoved her back.

"Okay," Colton said, reaching for Eli's shoulder and holding him back. "You going to let us in or what?"

The boys all ran off, leaving Layla and Joey behind. Layla was carefully watching Joey. Joey wished she wasn't standing so close. "You okay?" Layla asked.

"I'm fine. That's just Eli being Eli, I can take a hit."

"I know you can." Layla winked. "But I don't want us getting thrown out because you decide you need to hit back."

Joey shot her a look. She purposely rolled her eyes, pretending what Layla said didn't bother her. "Very funny. Come on, let's go in."

Joey hadn't gone to a party or hung out with all of her classmates in what felt like forever. Ever since she'd hit Danny with the soccer ball—or, well, even before that if she was being honest—she mostly just sat at the end of the lunch table with her brothers and Layla, minding her own business. Besides hockey, she hadn't been surrounded by this many kids outside of a classroom in ages.

She didn't realize, until she found it a little more difficult to breathe when she was surrounded by them, that it mattered.

Besides the boys from the hockey team, Joey saw girls from school, too. Aubrey and Sammi and Alexis immediately greeted Layla. They waved awkwardly when they noticed Joey was with her. Joey wasn't sure if she should wave back.

She felt her shoulders inch toward her ears and kept close to Layla. Layla didn't seem to notice anyone's discomfort as she told Sammi how much she loved her cowboy costume. Or maybe she was just pretending not to.

Joey sure noticed. They were all looking at Layla like they couldn't understand how she could be friends with Joey in the first place. It made Joey wonder what Layla was like at parties when Joey wasn't invited, if she stood with those girls and had more fun than if Joey was there.

Someone—maybe Jackson? Joey wasn't sure, thanks to the annoying Halloween masks—jumped out with a loud roar, making the girls scream. Layla jumped, letting out a nervous giggle, and Joey held her breath for a moment, hands fisting the fabric of her costume tightly. "Jerk," she mumbled.

Eli's parents were mostly out of the way, in the kitchen or living room or something, but she caught glimpses of them carrying bowls of chips and putting out soda bottles and cups. The party was mostly contained to the large dining room. The dining room table was pushed against the wall and being used as a buffet, pizza boxes from Timoney's Pizza spread out along it, leaving plenty of floor space to pack in sixth graders. There was a Bluetooth speaker in the corner of the room that was turned all the way up, and the music was loud, throbbing in Joey's ears.

The lights were all the way down except for some orange fairy lights strung around the room. With everyone wearing costumes (seriously, so many masks, and Joey hated masks), it was hard to see, well, anything. Joey was about to ask if they could go stand in another—brighter, quieter—room, when Layla suddenly grabbed her hand.

"Let's dance!" Layla said, tugging Joey into the center of the room. It was the very last place that Joey wanted to be.

But she wasn't going to *not* follow Layla.

Not when Layla's hand was soft and her smile was big and her eyes kept turning back at Joey to make sure she was still behind her, even though Layla hadn't let go yet.

Joey didn't really dance. She definitely hadn't inherited Mama's genes when it came to having any rhythm whatsoever. Or maybe she did have rhythm—she actually didn't know. She didn't like dancing, so she just didn't dance. She stood next to Layla while Layla danced in the center of the room, surrounded by classmates Joey barely knew, even though they had all been in school together for years. She was never very good at making friends even before they were all wary of her; Colton had befriended Layla first, and Joey was just always there, so suddenly they *were* friends, no making necessary.

Joey hadn't needed anybody else ever since.

Three songs later, it was almost a relief when Eli showed up out of nowhere shoving a slice of pizza in Joey's face. "Come on, we're having a competition. Everyone from the hockey team is in."

"A competition . . . eating pizza?" Joey asked.

"In one bite," Eli clarified.

Joey laughed. "Yeah, no."

"You're so *boring*," Eli said, and then slapped her across the face with the slice in his hand.

It didn't hurt—it was just pizza—but Joey felt the sauce dripping down her face and noticed how everyone stopped to look at her, including *Layla*, and the music was still *too freaking loud* and it was too dark, and he might as well have slapped her with his hand.

She felt Layla's hands on her arms, pulling her. "Joey, come on. Leave him. Let's go wash you up."

"What happened?" Thomas said, coming out of nowhere.

"Your sister can't take a joke," Eli said.

Joey was about to snap at him, but then Thomas asked, "Why, what'd Joey do?"

Joey turned to face him, pizza sauce all over her face, fists at her side. Of course Thomas assumed *she* was the one who did something.

Eli was laughing.

He was *always* laughing at her. Joey took a step toward him, wanting to get up in his face.

"Joey, just stop it," Thomas said, grabbing her arm and yanking her back. "Don't ruin the party."

"Get off me." Joey pushed Thomas off her. He stumbled back into someone else, who stumbled back into the table behind him, knocking over one of the soda bottles. It hit the ground, fizzy soda pouring out of it.

"Look what you did," Thomas accused.

"Joey—" Layla tried to reach for her again.

"That wasn't my fault!" Joey said, and it wasn't. Thomas didn't have to deal with Eli at hockey practice. He wasn't even in the same class with Eli, hadn't had to deal with him in gym or in class when he bumped her into walls and called her Bruiser.

She pointed a finger right at Thomas. "Why are you even here? You only get invited because you're Colton's and my brother. This is a hockey party. Get your own friends!"

Thomas's cheeks turned pink.

The whole spectacle delighted Eli.

"Woah, what's going on?" Colton asked, coming out of nowhere.

Pizza sauce was still dripping down Joey's chin. She wiped at it with her fingers, but then it was all over her hands and dripping down the collar of her costume.

Eli was now laughing at Thomas instead of her, and Colton was asking everyone what was happening, and the music was still too freaking loud.

A hand was suddenly in her own, even though hers was covered in pizza. "Come here, Joey. It's okay, you're fine. Let's go clean up," Layla said.

Colton looked down at their hands, and Joey felt the back of her neck get even warmer.

Layla tugged her gently out of the center of the room and over toward the table where Aubrey and the other girls were still standing. Aubrey quickly reached for the napkins to hand over to Joey. She met Aubrey's eyes as she took them. "Thanks," Joey mumbled.

"You're welcome," Aubrey said. "Do you need any more?"

What Joey needed was to leave this party. Her nose started burning. The last thing she wanted to do was let Eli make her cry. She shook her head. "I'm fine. It's fine."

"Eli shouldn't have done that," Layla said.

"Hey, let's go in the backyard," Alexis spoke up. "Eli has like a huge deck. We can get away from the boys for a little while."

"Grab the bowl of chips. It won't be as loud out there, either," Sammi said.

Aubrey grabbed the bowl of chips (and more napkins) and the three of them started walking out of the room to the back door. Layla went to follow them. She stopped when she turned to see that Joey was staying put. "Joey, are you okay? Are you coming?"

"I'm sorry," Joey said, feeling like she had to say it, because she was wrong, she was messed up, she couldn't even enjoy a party. No wonder she never got invited anywhere.

But Layla shook her head. "It's *okay*, Joey. Let's just go outside."

"They don't want me there," Joey said.

Layla sighed. "Nobody said that. And, anyway, *I* want you there. We're having fun. Don't let Eli ruin that."

Layla once again reached for Joey's hand.

She let Layla lead her outside.

12

Joey woke to a bunch of notifications on her phone. She'd been tagged in a whole lot of pictures from the night before. She scrolled through all of them. Most of the pictures were taken on the back deck. Everyone was smiling in them. Even Joey.

Being slapped with a slice of pizza aside, Joey had a good night. She didn't call Aubrey a rat or lash out at any of them. Not even when Sammi accidentally dumped the chip bowl all over her legs. "At least we ate all the good ones," Layla had said. "I wouldn't want to eat off of Joey's pants." Everyone had laughed. Even Joey.

They boys eventually came outside, too, and Jackson picked Joey first to be on his team for manhunt. "She's the fastest on the hockey team!" he said. None of the boys disagreed with him. Thomas avoided her, and Joey avoided Eli, and nothing went wrong the rest of the night. Joey didn't ruin anything.

The sun was poking through the curtain in her new bedroom, because the curtain was crooked, and Joey's mom was supposed to fix it, but hadn't yet. She climbed out from under her covers, bare feet padding across the carpeted floor as she yawned and slowly opened her door.

Across from her, the bathroom door was open, and she could see the back of one of her brothers' heads. From behind, sometimes even Joey couldn't tell them apart. But Colton had a way of slouching that Thomas didn't. Thomas, like Mama, had really good posture, so it must have been Colton, as he basically leaned his entire upper half against the bathroom sink, brushing his teeth.

(Joey couldn't help but wonder, suddenly, if the donor slouched. Colton didn't get mad, or at least not like Joey did, but Mama *never* slouched. All three of the triplets must have had to get something from their anonymous half, after all.)

Joey entered the bathroom and reached for her own toothbrush. Hers was blue. Colton got the pink one, because when her brothers tried to pawn it off on her just because she was a girl, she made a huge fuss about it. She reached over her brother for the toothpaste. "Last night was fun," she said.

Colton spit into the sink, rinsed off his toothbrush, and put it away. He met her eyes in the mirror. He frowned at her. "Really?"

"What? It was."

"Well, yeah. But you were kind of mean to Thomas," he said. "You're always kind of mean to Thomas. Everyone laughed at him, you know."

"Okay, but he blamed me for—"

"And what's with you and Layla, anyway?" Colton asked, pushing away from the sink. "Do you know she cried when you stopped talking to her? And now you're just . . . okay again? But whatever. That doesn't matter. Thomas was upset last night. And you know what? I'm kind of upset, too." He dried his hands on the towel and pushed past her to walk out of the bathroom, leaving her alone.

She didn't know what to say, so she didn't try to stop him.

Colton was always the first one to find her after she did something stupid. He'd never gotten upset with her before.

Joey looked at herself in the mirror and sighed.

It *had* been a good night.

Suddenly, Mama was standing at the threshold to the bathroom. Joey stayed where she was, watching both of their reflections as Mama leaned against the doorframe. They looked so much alike sometimes that Joey wondered if that was what she would look like when she got older. Just like Mama. Joey traced both of their noses with her eyes, before following along their similar lips and chins.

"Your mom and I want to talk to you downstairs, Jo-Jo," Mama said. She held out a hand.

Joey hesitated before taking it. "What about?" she asked.

Mama smiled softly at her. "Nothing bad. I promise."

Joey followed her downstairs, hand in hand. She sat on the living room couch with a mom on either side of her. They exchanged glances over her head, like they'd been doing so often lately. Joey kept her eyes down at her toes, squirming under their attention. Her mama had said it was nothing bad, but this sure felt like the beginning of a lecture.

"We wanted to discuss something with you," Mama began. "Your mom and I have been talking, a lot, about your behavior lately. We were thrilled you got invited to that party last night, but we just want to make sure that everything else stays on track."

Joey just nodded. She didn't really know what her moms were getting at.

"You've been acting out a lot lately, and it's our job to make sure that you, and your brothers, all have the support you need," Mama continued. "Benny's going to be staying with Luka for a while, so he can focus on his senior year and we can spend time figuring out what to do here."

Joey looked up at Mom, feeling like the wind had gotten knocked out of her. "I don't want Benny to stay at Luka's!"

"Neither do we, sweetheart, but we need to make some changes and respect your brother's need for space in the meantime. We also decided last night—"

"You talked about me while I was at the party?"

"We decided," Mama continued, "that we're going to be talking with your pediatrician and possibly set up a meeting with the counselor at your school."

Joey snorted. She couldn't help it. "Mr. Ladik is a joke. He makes us call him Dan-o."

"We need to start somewhere," Mama said.

"Yeah, but if even the kids think the guy's a joke, how's this getting us anywhere?" Mom finally spoke up. She stood up from the couch, pacing across the living room. "She's *twelve* now. She should know better."

Joey's chest was squeezing tight. She bit the inside of her cheek, hard. She was *not* going to cry. She was *not* going to get mad. "I didn't do anything! Mama, you promised this wasn't anything bad!"

"*Listen*," Mama said, raising her voice a bit. "*Both* of you. This *isn't* bad! This is about figuring out what's best for you, Joey, so that you can be happy. That's all we want. That's all we're talking about doing. Right? Steph, right?"

Mom wiped her hands down her face. "Yeah. Okay. Right."

"Okay, Joey?" Mama asked.

Joey nodded.

Even though she didn't think any of this would help anything.

<center>~~~~•</center>

Their first hockey game wasn't long after. Mom talked the entire car ride. Joey's stomach hurt too much to engage.

Don't mess up, don't mess up, don't mess up.

"Are you guys nervous?" Mama asked, turning around in the passenger seat of the car to look back at them.

"Nah," Colton said.

Joey shrugged.

"They've got nothing to be nervous about," Mom said, winking at them through the rearview mirror. "They're going to be great."

Yeah, Joey thought, leaning back in her seat. *Great.*

Her phone buzzed in her pocket.

It was Layla. Good luck today! Sorry I cant come, you and colton will kill it!

Joey stared at the phone for a moment before glancing over at Colton. He was sitting in the middle of the backseat, which was normally Joey's spot, leaning close to Thomas as they scrolled through something on his phone. Colton hadn't said much to Joey at all that day, and she tried not to think too much about it, because it just added to her stomachache.

They entered the gym, and Colton and Joey headed to go get ready while Thomas and their moms moved toward the bleachers. Joey, the only girl, got ready in the girls' locker room alone. She struggled still with tying her skates, but it wasn't like she could ask any of the boys for help with them, and she didn't want her mom to know she still hadn't learned how to do it right.

As she left the locker room, it struck her how loud it already was in the ice rink. She peeked around the corner to look at the bleachers. She found her moms, Thomas, and Benny, front and center. Benny had come with Luka, which made Joey feel weird, but at least he was there.

She tried to meet Mom's eyes. She wanted Mom to smile at her, to give her a thumbs-up, to make Joey feel like she could do this.

Someone suddenly bumped against her hard, almost knocking her over. "Hey, Bruiser." It was Eli, with Jackson right behind him.

Joey shoved Eli out of her face. Colton was standing right behind him. Joey was relieved to see him. But instead of standing beside her, or at least telling Eli to back off like he normally did, he walked right past her, heading for the bench with the rest of the team.

Joey sighed, picked up her stick, and tried to focus on the game.

The game started, and Joey waited, eagerly, on the bench.

And kept waiting.

She watched as her team went up against the opposition. Watched as the other team scored. Watched as Eli—because of course it was Eli—scored. Every time Luka came over to pull someone off the bench, Joey sat up straight and tall, hoping he'd notice her. He didn't. Which was okay, it was, it really was, until he finally gave Colton a turn to go in without her.

She turned to look at the bleachers, where her moms and brothers were cheering for Colton. It didn't matter that Joey was there.

She got up and moved to stand next to Luka. "Luka, come on. Can't I play?" she asked, glancing at the clock. There wasn't all that much time left.

Luka patted her on the shoulder. "Not this game. They're playing rough, and you're not great on keeping steady and strong on those skates yet. Give it time, Jo. Go sit down."

"But Luka—"

"It's Coach Cooper here," he said. "Go take a seat."

Joey turned and took her seat. Jackson, who had just gotten off the ice and was taking a drink of water, laughed. "Yeah, Bruiser. Keep that warm."

Joey stood back up to get in Jackson's face.

"Sit *down*, Joey," Luka said. His voice was as stern as when he yelled at Benny.

"You can't yell at me like that," Joey snapped. "You're not *my* dad."

He flinched a little, which made Joey feel good, because Luka was making all the hockey decisions and Luka got to keep Benny to himself and Luka once made a family with Joey's mom in ways that Joey couldn't. She'd seen the photographs that Benny still kept in his room, that even Luka still had on his mantel, of the three of them. "No, but I'm your coach. Sit down and watch the attitude. That's a warning, Jo. There won't be another one."

He turned his back on her, and even though she wanted to keep fighting, Joey took her seat. She ignored

Jackson and Eli and anyone else who talked to her for the rest of the game.

Her team scored, and she could hear her moms and Benny in the bleachers behind her, cheering louder than anyone else in the stands.

≈≈≈≈•

That night, Joey sucked it up and knocked on Thomas's bedroom door. She didn't wait for him to answer, just swung it open to find him sprawled on his stomach on his bed, playing a game on his cell phone. He looked up at her for a second before focusing back on his phone.

It was weird, how Thomas and Colton were exactly the same height and had nearly the same hair (Thomas's was a little shorter) and the same smile and teeth and nose and everything, but still, to Joey, they sometimes looked so different. She couldn't really explain it. She wasn't sure if it even had anything to do with their genes. She could picture Colton in her mind, doing the same thing Thomas was now, with his squinty eyes and set jaw as he played video games. Thomas's face was softer, his eyes wide, bottom lip tucked into his teeth.

Joey wondered what she would look like doing the same thing.

"Thomas?" Joey said. "I wanted to just . . . well, you know. Colton said you were upset about what I said at the party, and, well—"

Thomas pushed off his bed and walked over to his door. "I don't want to talk to you, Joey. You never mean it when you say sorry, anyway."

"Can you at least tell Colton that I tried?" Joey asked. "He's being weird about it."

Thomas raised his eyebrows, before motioning for her to get out of the way of the door that he was ready to close in her face.

"Come on, Thomas. Please," she said as she moved back into the hallway.

He closed the door.

At school on Monday, Colton was being extra grumpy in science while they worked on their projects. He was slumped over his desk, waiting for Layla to stop shuffling through her backpack.

"Shoot. Can I borrow a pen?" Layla asked him.

"Here, take mine," Joey said. She didn't plan on doing any writing, anyway.

"You need yours," Colton said, scowling. "You need to pull your weight on this project, too."

Layla pushed her seat closer to Joey. "It's fine. We can share." She smiled at Joey.

Joey smiled back before needing to look away. She met Colton's gaze instead. He was frowning. "What?" Joey said.

"You two have been weird and annoying to work with. I should have paired up with Jackson and Eli."

Layla crossed her arms over her chest, staring him down. "Well, no one's stopping you. You wanted to work with us."

Colton sat back in his chair, blinking at Layla for a moment, frowning even deeper. Joey decided to stay out of it. Especially when Colton stood, grabbing his backpack. "Fine," he mumbled. "I'm asking Mr. Hoover to switch."

Layla's eyes grew wide as he headed toward the front of the room. "Wait, Colton, we don't want you to—"

"Just leave him alone," Joey interrupted. "It's . . . sibling stuff. It's my fault. He says I'm mean to Thomas."

She sighed, bringing her chin down to rest on her desk. "I guess I *am* mean to Thomas."

"I don't think you mean to do the things you do sometimes," Layla said, which wasn't exactly what Joey wanted to hear. "Like how my mom can't control it when she gets anxiety attacks. Well, she couldn't, before she started seeing her doctor. You know, that's why we started the whole genealogy thing. My mom needed a project to feel good with. One minute we'd be shopping at the grocery store and the next she'd be telling me to call my dad to come get us."

"Your mom's not mean to you, though," Joey said.

"No," Layla said. "Well, she sometimes gets frustrated with me quickly? It's maybe not the same thing but . . . I don't know."

"Benny moved out because of me," Joey said, slumping low in her seat. "And my moms set up a meeting with Mr. Ladik. They don't know what to do with me."

"Oh, God, as if Dan-o is going to be any help." Layla laughed, and then got serious again. "Your moms love you, Joey."

Joey looked around the room, making sure Mr. Hoover was occupied elsewhere. Layla was jotting notes down on their worksheet, though Joey wasn't sure exactly what she was writing since they weren't discussing the project. Colton was now across the room.

"How easy do you think it would be for Mom to decide she doesn't want to be my mom?" Joey found herself asking.

Layla stopped writing. "Not easy at all. Like, colossally hard, because she's your mom, and she loves you."

"I mean logistically, since we're not biologically connected at all."

Layla's face scrunched up. "What are you even talking about? That's never mattered to you *or* her before. Is this about the 23andMe stuff?"

"Did I tell you that if there weren't three of us, Mom was going to have a baby with Mama, too, you know. Like, with her eggs or whatever." Joey found herself talking really quickly. "Benny left, and Mom—"

"Biology doesn't make a family," Layla said. "I've heard both your moms say that tons of times."

"I *know* biology doesn't make a family, Layla, but love does, and what happens if Mom falls out of love with me because I can't stop hurting everyone?"

"She wouldn't," Layla said. "No one could ever fall out of love with you. And you don't *hurt* people, Joey."

"Danny Carter?"

"That was an accident."

Was it? Joey didn't think she meant to hurt him, but she definitely meant to throw the ball as hard as she could at him. Wasn't that the same thing?

"It's getting a little loud in the back corner over there," Mr. Hoover said. "You should all be diligently working."

Joey and Layla fell quiet for a moment, and Joey's voice was lower as she said, "I don't know what's wrong with me. Mama never gets mad like me. Colton and Thomas *never* get mad like me."

"Colton gets pretty mad when his team loses during gym class."

"Not like me. Not like this. No one in my family gets like this."

"Okay, yeah, but that doesn't mean there isn't an answer for it," Layla said. "We just gotta find what that is. Here, look."

Layla slid over the notes she was working on. Joey took the worksheet from her and read it. There were columns: One for *Rebecca Sennett-Cooper*, one for *Stephanie Sennett-Cooper*, and one for *Unknown Donor*. Along the side of the paper, written down in rows:

Joey Sennett-Cooper, Thomas Sennett-Cooper, Colton Sennett-Cooper, Benny Cooper.

"What's this?" Joey asked.

"Our project. Nature versus nurture. We need a hypothesis, but I thought we could trace and compare all your traits and stuff with your moms. And, if we can find the donor . . ."

"I have money. From my birthday," Joey said. "Like you said."

Layla nodded. "I have money saved, too."

"We need Colton's help, though, you said? He just . . . left our group. And I don't want to tell him about this, anyway," Joey said.

Layla shrugged. "Leave that to me. I'll tell him we still need his saliva for our project or whatever. He'll do it."

Still, Joey hesitated.

Layla reached for Joey's hand. Joey held her breath. "There's nothing wrong with you, Joey. But yeah, maybe your donor has some sort of anger thing, too. Like my mom has anxiety. Maybe he knows what to do about it."

Joey picked up her pen, thinking. Under *hypothesis* she wrote: *You can figure out what makes a person who they are based on their genetic makeup.* Joey just knew she could find out what made her *her* once she found her donor. She glanced at Layla, but Layla didn't say anything.

"I'll give you the money tomorrow," Joey said. She forced a laugh. "Maybe we'll find out he's, like, some rich dude or something. That way if Mom decides she doesn't want me, I have a backup plan."

"Joey . . ." Layla said, eyes wide.

Joey waved her off. "I'm just kidding. It's just a joke."

But the first time in her entire life, she was wondering how real of a possibility that could be, after all.

13

The 23andMe results would take two to three weeks. Which meant that for two to three weeks, Joey would have to lay low, and be on her best behavior.

Which meant she would have to avoid Thomas. And Colton. And her moms.

She and Layla set up the 23andMe account. "Do you have an email address?" Layla asked.

Joey shook her head. "No. Just use my school one. We never use it." They were each given a school email address at the start of the school year so that teachers could reach their parents about issues and field trips and homework, but she didn't think she'd opened it once.

Layla filled out the account profile, and Joey couldn't believe how easy this was. They were supposed to be eighteen, unless they had a parent setting up the account for them, but Layla just clicked the buttons that swore they were old enough. "I'll just pretend I'm your parent, giving approval."

Layla swabbed Joey for her saliva (which was kind of gross—she had to basically suck on this foamy thing until it was soggy and then cap it into a tube—how Layla convinced Colton to do it, too, Joey had no idea). They "borrowed" stamps from Layla's dad's office to mail it off.

Two to three weeks. She just had to lay low until then.

Not long after, Thomas and Colton were getting ready to head to a free skate with a bunch of the other boys from school at the ice rink. Joey wasn't invited. It was, apparently, guys only, even though Thomas barely knew how to skate and Joey was the only one on the hockey team who wouldn't be going. Joey tried questioning Colton about it—she didn't really believe that no girls at all had been invited—but he wouldn't cave.

To top it all off, while the boys were off for their boys' night, Mama dragged Joey right out of her bedroom. "We can have our own girls' night! We never get to do that."

"Oh, hey, what's with the face, Little Growl?" Mom said. "Your moms are awesome to hang out with! Much more fun than skating around with a bunch of boys who haven't learned how to apply deodorant yet."

"Very true," Mama said. "I happen to think that I'm super fun."

"Sure you are, my love. Hey, what about going on one of those hikes you two seem to enjoy so much?" Mom asked.

Mama gathered Joey up into her arms. "No, that's a Mama and Joey thing. Get your own thing."

Joey stiffened. She wasn't prepared for her mama to hold her, she didn't want to be wrapped in Mama's arms. "Stop, let me go," Joey said, wiggling out of Mama's grip.

She accidentally elbowed Mama in the chest. Mama let out an *ooph*, letting go of Joey and bringing a hand up to rub at the sore spot. Joey froze, her body tense, realizing she hurt her.

"You okay?" Mom asked, alarmed, sitting up straighter on the couch.

Mama nodded. She coughed and cleared her throat. "Accidentally got me right in the rib cage. I'm good."

"You sure?" Mom asked, moving closer to Mama to rub her back.

Joey felt small, as if she wasn't in the room, even though she was standing in front of them.

"I'm fine," Mama said. "We've both got these boney string-bean arms. Sharp elbows."

Joey's throat hurt, her nose burned. She didn't want to cry in front of them, and she wasn't entirely sure she had a reason to. She didn't want to spend time with either of them anymore. "I'm just gonna go hang in my room," she said.

"No, stay, we'll watch a movie or something. I'm fine, really," Mama said.

Joey couldn't stop herself from saying, "I don't *want* to spend time with you."

Mama's face fell, and she looked more hurt from *this* than when Joey elbowed her.

"That's fine," Mom said. "We won't force you."

Joey kind of wanted them to force her.

But now Joey's chest squeezed tightly, and Joey couldn't stop. She never could, once she started. "And

I don't want to go on those annoying hikes anymore, either. You're the only one who likes them."

"Joey," Mom said, quiet but stern, and Joey chose to look at her, at the anger on Mom's face, instead of turning to see the hurt she was sure was on Mama's. "Just go ahead to your room."

Joey knew, she *knew*, that there was no reason why she should be saying these things, purposely hurting Mama more and more. She knew she didn't want to hurt Mama. She didn't, she *really* didn't. It was just . . . everything jammed up in her chest and sometimes if she just let it out things felt better. All she wanted was to feel better.

But this didn't feel good. Nothing about this felt good.

14

Two to three weeks later (it was sixteen days, Joey had counted) Layla texted her: The results came in. I'm waiting for you to look at them. Can you come over later today?

They had to wait an entire extra day, because Mom had work and Joey had kind of been avoiding one-on-one time with Mama since she'd hurt her feelings.

In the meantime, Joey's stomach was full of something stronger than butterflies, like Mothra or Mothman or something. She couldn't eat much that morning, which Mama noticed.

Mama didn't say anything though. She only asked, "Finished?"

Joey said, "Yeah."

And that was that.

Usually Mama would try her hardest to talk Joey into at least two more bites.

Everyone was walking on eggshells lately. The night before, Joey was in the bathroom brushing her teeth when she heard her moms talking. She turned off the sink to listen better, almost wishing they were back in the motel so she could hear more clearly, as Mama said, "Her pediatrician thinks it might be something worth discussing with a family therapist, instead of the school counselor. And, you know, I have to agree. I'm getting a little nervous around her, too, lately. I never know what's going to set her off."

Joey turned the sink on full blast, as hard as she could, even if that meant the water splashed all up the sink and onto her shirt. She didn't want to hear any more of it.

When she was finally able to get to Layla's, they had gone straight to Layla's room. Layla turned her laptop on. (She was the only person Joey knew who ever actually turned their laptop off, but Layla said the battery was better for it.) She got straight to work, turning the screen so Joey could see it. "Okay so, it can get a little confusing, but basically what we want to look at is this, your possible relatives based on the other DNA they have on record. Look, your mama's parents have a 23andMe profile, see? And we can trace a lot more through the research they've already done, to see other people you're related to through the Sennetts." Layla was talking a million miles a minute.

Joey wasn't entirely sure what she was looking at as Layla pulled her close. Layla smelled like her usual vanilla lotion. Joey wished she didn't have an empty stomach. She was feeling a little nauseous now. "It's not the Sennett side I need to find."

"No, I know. So, that's where these people come into play." Layla suddenly turned to face Joey, her head blocking the screen. "Look, before we actually dive into this, I need to ask . . . are you sure you want to do this?"

Joey was practically sweating. "Well, yeah. We paid all that money. And our project, and stuff."

"Joey," Layla said, sighing. "You know what I'm asking. Are you *sure*?"

"I said I'm sure," Joey snapped.

Layla slowly nodded. "These people? They're the ones not related to you on your Sennett side. Which means . . . well, they'd probably, well, they *are*, related to the donor. None are a paternal match or anything, I mean . . . they're not *him*. But it may take a little time. My mom and I have been doing this all year and we're still figuring out the links and history and connecting everyone." Layla motioned toward the family-tree map on her wall. Joey looked at the lines that connected Layla to her mom, and her dad. The branches that connected them with all of the rest of the people in her extended family. "We can keep tracing. We can even figure out if any of them are related directly to him, you know? Like, your grand-mother. I mean, not *your* grandmother. I know they aren't . . ."

"I know what you meant," Joey mumbled.

"We really don't need to do this," Layla said. "We can just . . . see if you're related to Vikings or some-thing. Maybe the queen! We don't need to do anything else with this."

Layla reached out to touch Joey's shoulder, but Joey pulled away. She didn't want Layla touching her. She didn't even know that she actually wanted to be here anymore right now. Joey couldn't take her eyes off the screen, off that stupid little map of people she apparently shared DNA with.

"I, um." Joey swallowed. It went down hard in her throat. "Can you text me the link for all of this?"

"Yeah, here. I'll send it now," Layla said.

Joey felt her phone buzz in her pocket as the text came through, and she reached over Layla to click the X in the corner of the screen, wanting to be done with the 23andMe page for now.

When Mom came to pick her up later before dinner, Joey's phone felt as heavy as a brick in her pocket.

~~~~~•

In school the next morning, Joey was struggling to focus on answering the questions Layla wrote in science class about her moms and brothers and herself. She hadn't slept well the night before, scrolling through her 23andMe page and looking at all the people she was supposedly connected to. Names of people she didn't know, faces she didn't recognize.

The most common last name that kept coming up

was Page. Joey wondered if that was the donor's last name. She wasn't really sure it mattered. It wasn't like it was *her* last name or anything.

She already had two last names. *Sennett*, for Mama. *Cooper*, for Mom.

Joey Sennett-Page, she suddenly thought, just to hear it in her head. Just to see how it sounded, to see if it fit any better.

"What about your mom?" Layla was saying, pulling Joey from her thoughts. "Thomas and her both laugh at the jokes they're telling before they finish telling it. Does that count? And you and her are both super stubborn."

"What? No," Joey said. "No."

"So stubborn! You and your mom are seriously like the same person that way. Like, oh my God, that time we played Monopoly when the power went out during that hurricane, and Colton got mad because you guys were playing wrong, which you were by the way, but you and your mom *refused* to admit it! Even after your mama got out the directions to read!"

"Layla, stop." Joey didn't want to do this. She didn't want to think about how she fit or didn't fit with her family. "I don't want to talk about this."

"Well, we kind of have to. This is our project."

"Well it's a stupid project!" Joey yelled.

"Joey," Mr. Hoover said, making his way across the room. "Is there a problem over here?"

"Yeah, your entire lesson is the problem," Joey said. "You don't know anything about genetics, you're just making this whole thing up as you go along. That's why you had us choose what we were gonna study in the first place."

"Joey, lower your voice, okay? I'm listening—"

Joey didn't let Mr. Hoover finish. "This is dumb, we know all of this stuff already! Lady Gaga sang an entire song about it, okay, we're *born* this way, period. Because of our biological moms and dads. That's how it works. That's why my mom doesn't know *anything* about me."

"Joey, what are you talking about?" It was Colton, but Joey didn't want to listen to him. He didn't know anything about her, either, and he didn't get to choose now to decide to talk to her again.

"Why don't we step out into the hall and talk about this," Mr. Hoover said. "It's clear you're upset about something, and I'd like to figure out what that is. I don't want this project hurting you."

"I don't *care* about the stupid project!" Joey yelled.

And before she even realized what she was doing, she was throwing her heavy science textbook at the classroom window.

15

Joey sat on the bench outside of the principal's office. The police officer that worked at the school stood next to her in his full uniform. Joey barely knew him. She saw him sometimes in the morning when he greeted them from outside the entrance. He walked around the halls during the day, so she occasionally walked past him. He was also the one who ran their many lockdown drills, so she knew his voice well.

He was always just there, like the rest of the teachers in the school Joey hadn't had and didn't know.

Now, though, as he stood next to her, watching her

(guarding her?), Joey was all too aware of him. She sank low in her seat, trying to make herself small, kind of afraid of him.

Mom wasn't here yet.

Joey kept thinking about how Colton told her Mama said they had been lucky the security guard at the old apartment hadn't called the cops. Joey hadn't touched anyone this time, though. She broke a window, and no one was hurt, but Mr. Hoover had escorted her to the principal, and the principal had called Officer Wilson before she'd even called Joey's mom.

Officer Wilson, when he showed up, didn't say anything to her other than "Sit there and don't move."

Joey glanced up at the clock. They'd been waiting a while. Mom was usually quicker than this when they needed her.

She was about to ask if Principal Porter could call again when Joey heard Mom, even before she saw her. She recognized Mom's quick, heavy footsteps and the jingling from the ring of keys she always wore attached to her work-uniform belt. Mom turned the corner and looked at Joey. Joey's hands were clamped tightly together in her lap, palms sweaty. The tighter she clasped her hands, the less they shook.

Mom looked over at Officer Wilson, before immediately reaching for Joey. "What's going on, are you okay, Joey?"

"Ma'am," Officer Wilson said, holding his hand out and blocking Mom's path to Joey. "Step back for a moment, please."

"Absolutely not, that's my kid," Mom said.

Officer Wilson looked from Mom to Joey and back at Mom again. Joey was used to that—she and Mom both were. They looked so different, and regardless of how normal adoptions and different types of families were, people still tended to wonder and judge. "You're her mother? I just need to confirm with Principal—"

"That's my *daughter*," Mom said, voice rising. "And she looks *terrified*. So, yeah, get Principal Porter right now while I have a minute to comfort my kid."

"She destroyed school property," Officer Wilson said. "From what I understand she was out of control, so Principal Porter asked me to sit with her to make sure—"

"Get the principal. *Now.*"

Joey wanted to cry. She knew her mom's anger was probably because of her, because Joey messed up, again, and Joey was in big trouble, *again*, and now Mom was fighting with a police officer because of it.

But Joey was just so relieved she showed up at all.

"What's going on? Oh, Mrs. Cooper, hi," Principal Porter said, as she opened her office door to see what the commotion was. "Why don't you come inside so we can talk, yeah?"

"Look, she's freaked out and she's a good kid, can we—"

"Good kids don't smash school windows," Officer Wilson said.

"Hey!" Mom snapped at him, and Joey flinched at the sound of it. "You don't know anything about my daughter."

"Mrs. Cooper!" Principal Porter held her door wide open.

"Sennett-Cooper," Mom corrected.

Principal Porter nodded. "I understand everyone is on edge right now. Why don't you come inside so we can fix that. Okay?"

Mom took a breath and nodded at her. She reached out, again, for Joey, gently grasping Joey's chin and lifting her face to meet hers. "I'll be right back, okay?"

Joey nodded. "Okay."

She was suspended. Which was better than being arrested, but still, it made Joey's stomach hurt. She didn't know *anyone* who got suspended. Sometimes kids got detentions for coming late all the time or never doing homework or talking back to the teacher. But Joey didn't know a single kid in her grade who ever got suspended.

Only the really, really bad kids got suspended. The older kids who had things they shouldn't have in their lockers. The ones who said things they shouldn't say and caused lockdowns. The really bad kids . . . and now Joey.

Mom hadn't yelled at her yet. She left Principal Porter's office, reached for Joey's hand, and pulled her close as they left the school without so much as a good-bye to Officer Wilson. She hadn't even called Mama yet. They got in the car, and Mom turned it on and adjusted the rearview mirror before backing out of her parking spot.

"Are you hungry?" Mom asked.

Joey opened her mouth and then closed it. She wasn't expecting that; she didn't know what to say.

Mom kept her eyes on the road. "You're missing your lunch period now, right?"

"Yeah," Joey said. It came out quiet and wobbly.

Mom glanced away from the road for a moment to look at Joey, patting Joey's thigh in that way she always did.

Joey didn't understand why her mom was offering her comfort.

"We've got a lot to talk about, Little Growl," she said. "But I've got you, okay? You can breathe now, you're okay."

Joey's chest still felt too tight to breathe normally, though. Mom pulled into the parking lot for Sissy's Diner, and Joey didn't understand why her mom wasn't just yelling at her. "Were they gonna arrest me?" Joey asked, as Mom opened her car door.

Mom took a deep breath and exhaled, hard, through her nose. "No. I know that scared you, and I'm sorry. They have protocols or whatever, since you did break school property and you have a history of . . . Anyway, you're twelve, and you shouldn't have to feel that way."

"I'm not hungry," Joey said, feeling small.

Mom opened Joey's car door and held out her hand. "Come sit with me anyway."

They were seated in a booth in the corner of the diner, and when the waitress came around to take their order, Joey got chicken fingers and cheese fries, even though she didn't think she wanted anything. She *was* hungry, her stomach gurgling, but she had butterflies swirling around in there as well.

Mom got a cup of coffee and chocolate chip pancakes. She winked at Joey, though her smile wasn't all that big. "Don't tell your mama I had chocolate for lunch."

It all felt so . . . normal.

Joey thought she might cry.

She blinked, and tears fell down her cheeks, and suddenly she *was* crying.

Mom reached across the table to take Joey's hand. "Your principal told me your science teacher said you got upset because of what you were doing in class. About genes and all that? They think maybe it has something to do with, well, us, I guess. Maybe, like, you're feeling a little embarrassed about all that DNA talk and how our family—"

"I'm not embarrassed," Joey said quickly.

"Then what is it, why are you so angry, Joey?" Mom said. "Because you are *so* angry, and I just . . . I can't understand it, and I'm trying to. And if it has to do with our family . . . Does it? Is that the root of all of this? God, you must have thrown that book so hard for it to break the window glass like that."

"It was a heavy book," Joey said.

Mom stared at her for a moment before she let out a bubble of laughter that startled Joey. Mom covered her mouth. "I'm sorry. I don't know why I'm laughing. I can't believe you just said that. This is serious. You're suspended!"

"I know that," Joey said, sinking lower in her seat.

The waitress came by with their food, and they fell quiet until she left. Joey looked down at her plate. She wasn't hungry again.

Mom checked her phone. "Mama's waiting for us at home. She's been talking about us all maybe going to see a doctor. A therapist, I guess."

Joey frowned. "All of us? Everyone?"

"Me, you, and Mama at first, and then, yeah, the boys, too," Mom said. "I gotta admit, Joey, I'm not entirely sure about it either. I don't like this whole . . . talking-to-a-stranger-about-our-problems . . . thing, you know? I don't really know how it'll work, but I'll give it a chance, for you. Mama thinks it might help, and I'll do whatever we need to do to get us help. I love you, Little Growl. No matter what."

"Only the really bad kids get suspended," Joey mumbled.

Mom stole one of Joey's fries and pointed it at her. "Well, we now know that *that's* not true. Eat your food, we'll talk more with Mama when we get home."

~~~~•

That conversation with both her moms ended up being shorter than she anticipated. The entire day after the window shattered had not gone like she expected it to. She expected yelling and slammed bedroom doors and punishments. She expected her mom, at least, to throw her hands up, to wave the towel and decide that enough was enough.

Instead, she got her mama explaining how Joey would be staying home with her for the next two weeks, but that didn't mean she would get a free pass to hang in her room and play on her phone and watch TV all day. Mama explained, too, that Joey's pediatrician put her in touch with a family psychologist that the three of them were going to go see next week. She told Joey that Joey was going to have to write a letter of apology to Mr. Hoover and to Principal Porter, and that when she got back to school, she would apologize to her class.

Her suspension meant that she would not be allowed to play hockey for the next two weeks, which was fine with her. She'd been dreading hockey practice. It wasn't bringing her any closer to her mom, and she hated listening to the boys call her Bruiser, the way they bumped and shoved her as they skated past. She hated the way Colton let them do all of it without saying anything.

"That's it?" Joey said when they were finished.

Mom's eyebrows rose. "You want more?"

"No, I just . . ." Joey shook her head.

"I should get dinner started then," Mama said, standing up and smiling tersely at Joey before leaving the room. Joey watched her go, until she disappeared around the corner. Mama hadn't been talking to her all that much lately, but it was different than the way Mom didn't talk to her when she was mad. Mama was just . . . quiet.

"She's mad at me," Joey said before Mom could leave the room, too.

"No." Mom shook her head. "She's hurt. I know sometimes maybe you don't mean the things you do, but the things you say can hurt. I sometimes feel like . . ." Mom paused, like she was going to add something more, but changed her mind.

Joey thought about that, and thought about all the apologies she just kept lining up. So many *I'm sorry*s.

Joey supposed it was time to start.

<center>~~~•~~~</center>

That night, while Mom was in the shower, Joey knocked on her moms' bedroom door. "Come in," Mama said. Joey found her sitting on her bed, lotioning her long legs. Thomas and Colton had long legs, too. Joey was still waiting for the growth spurt she always assumed she would have. Now, though, she was wondering if maybe the donor was short, and Joey got *his* legs, instead.

She didn't want to be thinking about that. Not right now.

"Hi," Joey said, which was a ridiculous thing to say and she immediately felt dumb for saying it. "Um, I just . . . wanted to tell you something."

Mama patted the spot next to her on the bed, but Joey didn't move from the door. "What's up, Jo-Jo?"

"I do like taking walks with you," Joey said, even though it was kind of a lie. Saying she hated it was a lie, too. She didn't care about the hike, not like Mama did. She didn't care about the view at the top that made her want to scream as loud as she could instead of enjoying the peace. But she did care about being with Mama. "So, if you want to go again, sometime . . ."

"It's starting to get colder out," Mama said.

Joey swallowed the lump in her throat. Her nose burned; she felt like she might cry. "Then we should go soon?"

Mama put the lotion down on her nightstand and quickly got off the bed to make her way over to Joey. She wrapped her arms around Joey, hugging her tight. "Yes. I'd love that. I'd love to keep walking with you."

Joey had been on edge the whole day. In her

Mama's arms, she could breathe, and finally felt herself relaxing.

In bed that night, Joey cradled her cell phone in her
hands, her 23andMe profile page pulled up. She stared
at it, thinking about the unknown man that shared half
of Joey and her brothers' DNA. The unknown man
who was related, probably, to the people who were
connected to Joey but who weren't connected to her
through Mama.

She could pick any one of them right now and write
them an email. She could ask any one of them if they
ever got angry. She could ask them to tell her everything they knew about themselves, or if they knew who
in their family was maybe her donor, so she could write
down every bit of information possible on her worksheet for her science project. So she could see what
traits they all shared.

Joey opened up her inbox.

Dear Mr. Page, she wrote, even though she still
didn't know who he was—if he was even Mr. Page at
all—or where to send it. *My name is Joey and me and
my brothers were made with half of your DNA. Can you*

roll your tongue? Is your second toe longer than your big toe? Are your earlobes attached? I'm writing because I'm doing a project in science class about biology and genes. Also, I really need to know if you ever feel really, really mad for no reason. This is very important, so if you could write me back and let me know that would be very nice of you. If you do feel very, very mad sometimes, I also need to know what you do to stop it. Thank you, Sincerely, Joey Sennett-Cooper.

Joey needed to find where to send it. She needed to ask Layla to help her sort through all her relatives on the not-Sennett side, on the maybe-Page side. She needed these answers, and fast.

Right?

Joey thought that was what she needed. But she kept going back to how nice it felt being in her mama's arms. She thought about how her moms were going to go to therapy with her, even though Joey was nervous about that, even though Mom didn't seem entirely too thrilled about it, either. She thought about how Mom could have yelled and screamed and given up on Joey for breaking the window. How Mom defended her to Officer Wilson.

How her mom showed up to get her at all.

Maybe 23andMe could wait.

Joey kept the email in her drafts, put the phone on her dresser, and rolled over to try and sleep.

16

In the world's most awkward scenario, Joey's moms made her go to the next hockey game with them. They made her sit in the bleachers and cheer for her team, because "even though you can't play, you made a commitment, and should be there to support them."

Well, that was Mama's position anyway.

Even more awkward, she ended up sitting next to Thomas. It felt deliberate. When she'd been about to take a seat next to Mama, Mom had grabbed the back of her shirt and said, "Let me sit next to my woman," and then snuggled up close to Mama.

When the game started, Joey watched her team take the ice. Mom *woohoo*ed really loud in Joey's ear any time her team made a good play. Joey scooted a little away from her, but then she bumped into Thomas, who in turn scooted away from Joey.

Benny was sitting on the other side of Mama, and Mom kept leaning over her to ask him questions she would normally ask after school or over dinner—moments that had been so normal for the first twelve years of Joey's life but lately didn't include Benny at all. Once a week he came over for dinner, and he made it to all of the hockey games, but they didn't see him much else, otherwise.

"What about homecoming?" Mom was asking. "Are you going? Are you taking someone? Can you get ready at our house so I can see you and take photos?"

Benny squirmed in his seat. "What? Maybe. I don't know. I might go with my friend Charlotte."

"Who's Charlotte?" Mom asked. "Do we know Charlotte?"

"Can we just watch the game?" Benny said.

"Make sure you find out what color dress she's wearing so we can get a good corsage to match," Mama chimed in.

Benny groaned. "I don't even know if we're going yet, Mama."

"Well, when you do know, maybe you can actually let us know," Mom said, her voice getting a little tense in a way Joey recognized. "God forbid you let your mothers be part of your life anymore."

"Seriously? Mom, really?"

Mama lightly grasped his shoulder. "We just miss you, Bubba, that's all."

Joey tried to tune them out and focus on the game, but she didn't like watching Colton and Eli and Jackson play like a team. She didn't know how she felt about Colton being friends with them. She felt like she was losing all of her brothers in one fell swoop.

Joey had hurt Thomas's feelings, yes. But Thomas and Colton had hurt her feelings, too. Eli had hit her across the face with a piece of pizza, he'd pushed her into walls, he'd called her Bruiser—and neither of them said *anything*.

Mama made a noise and shivered dramatically. She rubbed her hands together. "It's always so cold in here."

"It's a hockey rink, my love," Mom said, rolling her eyes. She reached into her pocket to pull out her wallet, handing Joey some cash. "You and Thomas go get your mama some hot cocoa."

"Alone?" Mama chimed in. "Benny, go with them."

"I can see the snack bar from here, they'll be fine by themselves," Mom said.

Joey turned to look at Thomas. He didn't look all that thrilled.

Joey sighed and pocketed the money. "Come on, let's go."

She stood next to Thomas on the line for the snack bar, neither one of them saying anything. Thomas kept his eyes straight on the back of the head of the person in front of him. Joey tried to do the same, but couldn't help looking over at him. It made her think about all the names on her 23andMe account, all of the supposed relatives they were connected to. If she found their donor among them, would he look like Thomas and Colton? Like Joey?

The triplets all had long, thick eyelashes. Joey always assumed that they got that from Mama, but were Mama's only long and thick because she wore mascara? Thomas moved his shoulder to rub it against his chin, something he did when he had an itch, and Joey wondered if any of the donor's relatives did that, too. Mama didn't.

Mama's hair was a tad darker than the triplets.

And when they were little, their moms had all three of them grow their hair longer because of a cowlick they couldn't make stay down. Mama didn't have that cowlick. Did the Page-family side?

"Stop staring at me, Joey," Thomas said, his voice quiet even though he sounded annoyed.

"Sorry," she mumbled, as they moved closer to the register. "Hey, Thomas?"

Thomas sighed and kept his face forward.

"I didn't mean to make you get laughed at on Halloween. You have to know that. Eli was being, well, *Eli*, and I just . . . You know?"

Thomas shrugged.

"I really didn't mean to."

"Maybe not at the party, but you're always mean to me, Joey," Thomas said.

The woman at the register called, "Next!" Thomas stepped up to the counter to order five hot chocolates, handing the woman the money that Mom had given them. She gave him a carrier, which he took, leaving Joey empty-handed.

Thomas started walking back toward their parents, but Joey reached for his sleeve to pull him back. He flinched, and Joey let go. "Sorry," she said again. "I just . . . what if I told you I might have thought of a way to fix things. So maybe I won't be so mean anymore."

"Moms told me they were gonna take us all to therapy, if that's what you mean," Thomas said.

"Not that," Joey said. "Something else. Would that make a difference?"

Thomas shook his head and started walking again toward the bleachers. "I don't know, Joey, can we just—"

"I've been looking for our donor," she interrupted him.

He turned and faced her—eyes wide and forehead wrinkled—for the first time in weeks.

~·~~·~~·~~·~~·~

Immediately after they got home from the hockey game, Thomas pulled Colton into Joey's room. Colton had no idea what was going on. He looked back and forth between his siblings. "What happened? Did something happen?"

"Let Joey tell you," Thomas said. He stood by the door, as if he wanted to make a quick getaway, with his arms crossed. When he glanced down the hall, Joey realized he was keeping an eye out for their moms.

"What'd you do?" Colton asked, which made Joey's stomach flip, made her clench her jaw. Colton shrugged, as if it didn't matter what Joey did, anyway, and that was worse than Benny's sudden absence, it was worse than Thomas's avoidance. Colton had never brushed her off, not like this, and it *hurt*. "I need to shower, can we do this quick?"

Joey didn't know where to start. Or how. "You know how Layla and I were gonna do our family for the science project?"

Colton groaned. "Seriously? This is about schoolwork? About you and Layla, *again*?"

"What do you mean about me and Layla again?"

"It's not about schoolwork," Thomas interrupted, before looking pointedly at Joey. "*Tell* him."

"Well, we decided that we wanted to . . ." Joey paused. She couldn't lie to Colton and say this was all about the project. It wasn't. That was the point. "We've been looking for the donor. Layla and me, I mean. Because I asked her to."

Colton's eyebrows flew up. "You what? You and Layla are *what*? And she didn't tell me? You didn't tell me? Why would you . . . *how* are you . . . oh my God, is *that* why she needed my saliva—"

"Slow down," Joey said as Thomas shut the bedroom door, which was probably for the best. Colton wasn't exactly being quiet—he always got louder when he got excited or nervous. "Yes. That's why we needed your saliva. Layla didn't tell you because I told her not to. I didn't tell you because . . . I need to find him for me. We set up a 23andMe account, and there's all sorts of relatives, I guess, or whatever, that came up—"

"Oh my God," Colton said, taking a seat at Joey's desk chair. "I don't want to know this. I can't believe you tricked me into that. I don't want to know any of this."

"Have you like . . . talked to any of them?" Thomas asked.

"To who? They're strangers!" Colton practically yelled, causing both Joey and Thomas to shush him.

"I didn't do anything yet," Joey admitted. "Mom was so weirdly nice to me after I got suspended, I couldn't."

Colton was shaking his head. "Don't."

"Yeah, I mean, what if you reach out and then this, like, whole family of people we don't know try to . . . I don't even know. They're not our *family*," Thomas said. "You should have asked moms about this. You think they'd get upset if they knew? They'd definitely get upset if they knew. Mom hates talking about this."

"They both told me it's okay to be curious," Joey said defensively.

"Why are you even doing this? This isn't just about you, Joey," Colton said, standing up from the chair and pacing again. "Did you even think about Thomas and me?"

Joey felt the familiar feeling bubbling up in her chest, making everything feel tight, making it harder and harder to breathe. "Yes, Colton, I did! It's like what we're learning in Mr. Hoover's class. If I can find the donor, I can figure out all of our genes, okay, I can figure out why I am the way I am!"

Thomas and Colton got quiet. Colton glanced at Joey's phone. He reached for it but stopped at the last second and didn't take it, didn't look. "I don't know," he said.

Joey picked the phone up, opening up her page on 23andMe and holding it out to her brothers.

Thomas shook his head. "I don't like this. This is so . . . weird. It's making me feel really weird. We should talk to moms about this," he said.

"*No!*" Joey snapped, but when Thomas's eyes grew wide again, she took a deep breath. "I mean," she said, quieter this time, "I just need time to . . . Please, just . . . don't tell them. I won't reach out to any of them or anything, not yet, I promise."

Thomas and Colton looked at one another. "Okay," Colton said, even though Thomas looked like he was going to keep protesting. "But seriously, Joey. You can't do anything without telling us first."

Joey's bedroom door suddenly swung open, and the triplets turned quickly to face it. Mom poked her head in, her eyebrows furrowed in confusion as she looked at them all. "Okay . . . what's going on?"

"Nothing," they all mumbled together.

One of Mom's pale eyebrows rose. "Alright. I was just coming to say that dinner's almost ready, so wash up and head down, okay?"

Mom paused for a moment, watching them. Joey hoped neither of her brothers would give them away; they were all such terrible liars. But finally, before anyone could say something, Mom ducked back out the door. Thomas glanced over at Colton and Joey before following her.

With Thomas gone, Colton looked Joey up and

down before saying, "Do you really think that could help? Finding the donor? Like, help you, I mean?"

Joey shrugged. "What if he gets really mad like me? What if he knows how to stop it?"

Colton shifted his weight from one foot to the other, his eyes squinting hard at the carpet. "I think it's better when he doesn't feel like an actual guy. Like it's just some weird thing that happened and then Mama was just pregnant and it doesn't matter how. I don't like thinking that he's . . . real."

"I know," Joey said, because she did. "But I really need this."

Colton nodded, still looking down at the floor. He turned to leave Joey's bedroom.

Joey's phone buzzed in her hands. It was a text from Layla—a link that read *click this!*

Joey clicked it, and it brought her to a web page that had a picture of Joey's head on top of a cartoon hockey player, skating around chasing a puck. Animated text flashed over the top of it, saying, *When you can play again in two weeks, they won't know what hit them!*

Joey smiled.

"What're you smiling at?" Colton asked.

Joey hadn't realized he was still standing there.

She showed him her phone. "Layla sent me this."

Colton looked at it. "Cute," he said.

He fell quiet but stayed in Joey's room. He opened his mouth to say something . . . but didn't.

"What?" Joey asked.

"You and Layla . . ."

"Yeah, we're friends again."

"No, I mean . . ." Colton shook his head. "Do you . . . like . . . Layla?"

Joey felt the heat in her cheeks. "Of course I do, Colton, she's my best friend, too."

Colton rolled his eyes. "I mean do you like her like Mom and Mama like each other. Like more than a friend. You always . . ."

"I always *what*?" Joey asked, voice high, getting defensive.

Colton held up his hands. "Relax. It's fine if you do. I think. I just . . ."

"You just *what*?"

Colton grew quiet again. He didn't look at her as he mumbled, "She's my friend, too. When you wouldn't talk to her, *we* did everything together. Layla and me." Colton shrugged. "It's like she doesn't want to hang with just me anymore, now that she has you back."

"Oh," Joey said. "I didn't know."

"Hey! Colton, Joey!" Mama's voice called from downstairs. "Dinner's up!"

Colton squinted at her, in that way he did when he was really, really trying to figure something out, and Joey wished he would stop. "Look, she still is my best friend, no matter what, and if you like her . . . well, okay. But don't, you know, hurt her, Joey. You already hurt her bad when you stopped talking to her. Just . . . don't do it again."

Joey nodded, and Colton turned to walk out the door.

When Joey had stopped talking to Layla, *not* hurting her was exactly what she was trying to do.

But what if she hurt Layla again? Colton already felt like Joey took Layla away from him, and here he was, asking her not to hurt Layla again, but what if Joey couldn't control that?

She didn't know what Layla would do if Joey told her that she liked her as more than a friend. As far as she knew, Layla was straight, so what if things went really badly? What if Joey just kept messing everything up?

Would she lose Layla and Colton for good? Just like she was losing Benny, losing Mom, losing everyone?

Joey looked back down at her phone, X-ing out of the link Layla sent her.

She wouldn't tell Layla a *thing* about her feelings.

It wasn't worth the risk.

17

Joey felt about two inches tall and a thousand degrees hot as she sat between her moms on a stranger's couch as they talked about, well . . . exclusively about Joey.

It wasn't really just a stranger. It was a therapist, hand chosen by Mama with help from Joey's pediatrician. Someone who, according to Mama, "specialized in children and blended families."

Joey knew how this worked; she watched a lot of TV. The therapist would ask questions, and her moms would answer them, and Joey would answer them, and they would try to find the root of the problem by figuring out some trauma from Joey's life that was the cause of everything. Only, Joey didn't *have* any trauma, did she? That's what Mom kept saying: that Joey had a good life and no reason to be this angry.

How on earth was this therapist going to be able to tell them any different in an hour, anyway?

Joey's chest felt tight, her shoulders were stiff, and she felt a little like she did during hockey practice when she was face-to-face with an opponent. Like she had a split second to decide if she'd be able to block them and get the puck or have to check them hard into a wall or something.

The couch wasn't even comfortable. Joey started thinking about everyone who had sat on it before her, all the other patients this therapist had, and she cringed. *Gross.*

"Why don't we start with the suspension," the therapist said. Her name was Dr. Cynthia Collins, and she seemed nice enough. She kind of reminded Joey of a mom, and she wondered if Dr. Collins had kids, too. If she had her own blended family, and that was the reason she decided to focus on them.

Joey looked around the room, trying to find some evidence of Dr. Cynthia Collins's life, but didn't see any family photos or anything, though she couldn't see everything that was on Dr. Collins's desk. Her office just looked like a boring office.

"Joey was suspended because she threw her science book through a window," Mama said. "Her science teacher said she got angry with him over the assignment they were working on. They're doing a genetics unit. The school has assured me that it's as inclusive as possible, but we think that it might be affecting Joey."

"Why don't you tell us about that, Joey?" Dr. Collins said. "How does studying genetics make you feel? Does it make you feel excluded? Different? Tell me about that, and about your family."

Joey narrowed her eyes. She was trying so hard to figure herself out, how could Dr. Collins possibly figure her out? How much had her moms told Dr. Collins, anyway? This wasn't about feeling different. Joey *was* different, and it wasn't because she had two moms, but also it *was*. Because there was a whole part of her she didn't know and understand, and maybe someone out there did. Maybe the donor *did*.

But it wasn't like she could tell Dr. Collins that she was looking for the donor.

And she sure as heck couldn't tell Dr. Collins that when she thought about the day she threw that book out the window, what she mostly remembered was sitting with Officer Wilson, waiting for her mom, wondering if she would show up at all.

Joey shook her head. "I don't want to talk about that. It's not like you can do anything about it anyway."

"Joey . . ." Mom warned.

"No, it's okay," Dr. Collins said. "This is new for Joey, and for the both of you. It's okay to feel hesitant and uncomfortable. It might take a bit for you to trust me, Joey, but you can trust that this room is safe. Your moms are here to listen, and I'm here to help with that. No, I can't wave a wand and get you unsuspended, but I can help you sort through the feelings that got you here in the first place."

The last thing Joey wanted was to sit here, sorting out her feelings in front of her moms. "But why? This is stupid," she said.

"Hey," Mom said, reaching for Joey's leg. "We talked about this, yeah? We said we'd give this a shot."

"Yeah but you said you didn't think it'd work, either," Joey snapped at her.

"Excuse me?" Mama said, shooting Mom a look.

Mom looked back and forth from Mama to Dr. Collins. "That's not . . . I told her I wasn't sure about this. Which I'm not! I just wanted to be honest. But I said that, for her, we'd try it."

"That's great, Steph," Mama said, crossing her arms over her chest and leaning back into the couch. "Real nice."

"Being here, being honest and open and willing to try," Dr. Collins stepped in, "is a good thing. There's nothing wrong with having opinions."

"But how is this going to work if you convince our daughter that it's not going to?" Mama asked. "We aren't going to be able to find the root problem if you're not willing to admit that there *is* a root problem! Your solution is, what? Just to keep grounding her?"

Mom looked over at Dr. Collins as if to say, *Back me up here, please.* "I didn't say that. I just feel like she knows she can talk to us, we talk all the time. Talking isn't the problem here."

"Clearly it is, if we can't even agree on what to do about this."

Great, Joey thought. Her moms were now fighting because of her. She felt even smaller than she had when they started.

"Okay, why don't we try to refocus," Dr. Collins said. She was looking at Joey. "Joey, I'd like to hear a little more from you."

Joey shook her head. "Why?"

"Because you're why we're here," Mom said, sounding exasperated. Both of Joey's moms were sitting stiffly, leaning away from one another.

This wasn't making things any better.

"How much longer do we need to do this?" Joey asked.

Dr. Collins didn't get mad at Joey for being a brat, and Joey kind of wished she would. She wished Dr. Collins would yell and lecture her. Joey wondered what it would take. She wondered if she could push all of Dr. Collins's buttons until she lost her cool, too.

"I want you to know that you are brave for being here, Joey, especially since you aren't thrilled about it," Dr. Collins said, and Joey scoffed. "I'll never force you to be here against your will. So, if you don't want to stay anymore, why don't you go wait outside in the waiting room so I can have a word alone with your moms?"

Joey stared at Dr. Collins, making sure this wasn't some sort of test. Dr. Collins didn't waver, though, and Joey's moms didn't object. "Whatever," Joey said, getting up and heading for the door.

Before she closed it behind her, she heard Mom say, thick with sarcasm: "Well, that went just great."

Joey felt exactly the same.

Joey pretty much stayed in her bedroom for the rest of the day. She could hear her moms bickering in their bedroom and tried her best to ignore it. Colton and Thomas kept their distance, too. Dinner was quiet and awkward; Mama asked Thomas to pass her the string beans even though Mom was closer. Mom left the table before she finished, putting her dish in the sink—leaving it there dirty, which Mama hated—and went upstairs.

Joey and her brothers helped Mama clear the table, and once the dishes were done, Mama disappeared upstairs, too. Colton kept glancing at Joey, but she wasn't going to tell him anything. Not about the therapy session, not about how their moms' fighting was all her fault.

When they were little, anytime their moms fought, Colton would climb into Joey's bed. He'd ramble on and on. He'd talk about school and about homework and about whatever he watched on TV that day, whatever popped into his head. He once spent an entire mom-fight talking about how he just found out that Jell-O was made out of horse bones. Joey wasn't sure if Colton did it to make her feel better or him feel better, but it always drowned out the sounds of their moms' fights, at least. Sometimes Thomas would join them, sometimes Benny would come in and make sure they were all okay. The four of them would try to stay up as long as they could, wanting to make sure their moms made up before they fell asleep.

Joey was alone tonight, though. Colton didn't come, Benny wasn't living at home, and it wasn't like she and Thomas had ever been close enough to comfort each other. Still, every time the floor creaked outside her door, she held her breath, hoping it was any one of them.

Joey was pretty sure she broke her and Colton, broke all her brothers, just like she broke the school window and just like maybe she was breaking her moms, too.

Joey took out her phone and logged in to her 23andMe account. She pulled up the email draft to her still-unknown donor. She started a new email to another unknown relative 23andMe said she was connected to. She wrote another, and another, to strangers Joey didn't know, but could know, now, if she wanted. They could know her, if she wanted.

They could maybe tell her that her feelings were normal, that she was okay, that they understood why she got so angry all the time.

Joey's phone buzzed in her hands, and she jumped as if the phone was possessed. She closed the emails without sending, leaving them in her drafts, and looked to see who was texting her.

It was Layla. Colton said things are weird at home. You ok?

Joey sighed. She didn't like to think about Colton texting Layla about how awful Joey was, but she was glad they were texting. She had been feeling bad about Colton thinking she was stealing Layla from him.

Moms took me to therapy and I hated it and now they are fighting.

Im sorry, Layla responded. What was therapy like?

Weird. Dr. Collins was fine I guess. She thinks Mr. Hoover's science class makes me feel different or whatever. I didn't tell her about the 23andme stuff. Joey sent it and then thought for a moment before adding, Does your mom see a therapist?

Yeah, Layla texted. She doesn't talk to me about it though.

Joey didn't know if that bothered Layla, but she could understand why Layla's mom maybe didn't like talking about it. Joey wasn't sure *she* liked talking to Layla about it. She kicked her blanket off, feeling a little too warm.

Her phone buzzed as another text from Layla came in: You can talk to me about it though if you want?

Joey didn't know how to respond. She kept thinking about what Colton said, about not hurting Layla. She thought about how she felt about Layla. She thought about how uncomfortable therapy made her, how uncomfortable all of this made her, and how she didn't want Layla to feel uncomfortable about her, too.

Joey's phone buzzed again, before she had a chance to reply. Even if you don't want to talk about it Im glad were friends again, Layla wrote.

Joey, despite everything, couldn't help but smile. Me too.

18

They were having the kind of lazy Saturday that felt more like everyone was avoiding talking to one another, rather than basking in a comfortable silence and enjoying the weekend.

Mama sat at the kitchen table with her laptop, saying she had work to catch up on, instead of lying with Mom on the couch. Thomas was in his room playing video games. Mom, Joey, and Colton were watching *Chopped* on TV. Usually they would each pick a contestant they thought would win, having a competition of their own. Today, though, they barely acknowledged they were watching together at all. Mom had called

Benny to ask if he wanted to spend the day with them, but he said he had plans.

Joey tried to think if she had said anything at all that morning. She wondered how long she could go without speaking.

Colton and Joey's cell phones both buzzed at the same time, the sound echoing as the phones vibrated on the wood of the coffee table. They both reached out to see who was texting them.

Joey made a face when she saw it was a group text from Jackson.

Colton spoke up first. "Jackson says he's having the hockey team over his house for a movie night. Can we go? He said we can bring whoever, so Thomas can come, too, if he wants."

Mom looked over at Joey. "That the text you got, too?"

Joey nodded.

"Do you want to go?" Mom asked her.

Joey wasn't sure. She was starting to kind of hate Eli and Jackson and the hockey guys. Staying home, though, while her moms played this weird "we're not fighting, we're just not *not* fighting" game didn't sound like a great idea, either.

She shrugged.

Mom motioned to the other room. "Go make sure it's okay with your mama, and go ask Thomas if he wants to go, too. Tell Mama I'll drive."

Tell her yourself, Joey wanted to say.

Joey turned to Colton instead. "You should invite Layla," she said, because she wanted Layla to go, and she wanted Colton to feel like he wasn't being left out.

"Okay," Colton said.

He left the room and Mom held out her hand. "Come here," she said, and Joey moved closer. Mom pulled her to stand between her legs, nice and close. "I know we've got a lot going on, but maybe a night out with your friends will be good, considering the past couple days we've had. Just do me a favor and be your best, okay?"

"She'll be fine," Mama said, entering the living room. "Won't you, Jo-Jo?"

Joey wasn't sure what was worse. Mom's need to give Joey a lecture before she went to hang with her friends, or Mama's conviction that Joey wouldn't get in trouble. Both felt impossibly heavy on her shoulders.

The boys came downstairs, and before Joey could

open her mouth, it was decided they were all going, picking up Layla on the way.

It wasn't like anyone was listening to Joey, anyway. They climbed into Mom's car to head to yet another party that Joey maybe wished she wasn't invited to at all.

When they pulled up in front of Jackson's house, and Thomas, Colton, and Layla all started unbuckling and climbing out of Mom's car, Joey didn't move. Mom noticed, glancing at Joey through the rearview mirror. Joey kind of wanted a pep talk. Mom didn't give her one.

"You call if you need anything," Mom said. "You hear me?"

Joey nodded, unbuckling her seatbelt, even though she knew she wouldn't call Mom if something happened. That was the job of the parents or principals or security guards, like it always was, after Joey did something. The best Joey could do was lay low. It was a movie night, right? She could sit in the corner of Jackson's living room, watch the movie, and keep to herself.

Joey used her brothers' height to keep herself out of the spotlight as they walked into Jackson's house, took off their jackets, and hung them in Jackson's closet. Layla seemed to notice, and she kept close. Close enough that Joey could smell her vanilla lotion. Joey mostly wasn't focused on Layla, though. She was too busy scanning the room for Eli.

"Do you see Eli anywhere?" Joey whispered to Layla as everyone gathered into Jackson's living room. There were a lot of kids smooshed together on Jackson's couches and on the carpeted floor. All the boys from the hockey team were there, along with a handful of girls from school, too. Nearly as many kids as were at Eli's party. Joey was sweating. At least there wasn't loud music, and the lights were bright.

"Jackson!" Layla called, grabbing him by the shirt-sleeve as he walked past them. "Is Eli here?"

Jackson shook his head. "He had a family thing tonight."

Hearing that, Joey felt like she could actually breathe. Layla noticed. "You know, you should tell someone that Eli upsets you. Your moms, even. He's kind of . . . well, a bully."

Joey shook her head. The last thing she needed to

do was call someone *else* a bully. Not when she knew what everyone thought of her.

Joey started to head toward the back of the living room where no one else was sitting, behind the couches everyone else was crowding around. Layla was right behind her. "You should go sit with Colton," Joey said. "He invited you."

"Well, yeah, but—"

Joey didn't wait for her to finish. She walked away and sat against the back wall, far away from everyone else.

Layla followed her anyway.

Jackson's mom had popped a ton of popcorn that she passed around in big bowls while Jackson and his dad messed around with the DVD player. "We always just watch Netflix or whatever," Jackson said with a shrug. "We like never use the DVD player."

Jackson wanted to show the hockey team *The Mighty Ducks*, some old hockey movie he was apparently obsessed with. Joey was pretty sure it had to be streaming *somewhere*, but Jackson's dad had it on DVD and was determined to use it. Jackson let out a loud *whoop!* when they finally got it to play. Jackson's dad turned the lights down as he left the room. There were a few shushes when the movie started, but basically everyone ignored them. Jackson turned the TV volume way up.

Joey sat with Layla, both of them leaning against the wall. Part of the couch was blocking their view of the TV, but Joey didn't really care about watching the movie, and Layla didn't seem to mind.

Joey pulled her knees into her chest, wrapping her arms around them to hold herself tight. She could do this. She could sit here with Layla, watch a movie, and keep to herself until it was time to go home. Maybe she could just . . . mind her own business and do some of Mama's breathing techniques or whatever.

Layla had managed to snag one of the bowls of popcorn. She sat it in her lap, and leaned over to whisper loudly, "Colton told me you told him and Thomas about the 23andMe account. A heads-up would've been nice, he's kinda mad at me for not telling him."

Joey swallowed. She couldn't talk about that right now. "He feels left out lately. Which is why you should be sitting with him and not me."

"But I want to sit with you."

"Let's just watch the movie, then," Joey said.

"Do you really care about this movie?" Layla asked.

Joey shook her head. "No, I just—"

"I wanted to ask you something," Layla quickly interrupted.

There was a bit of a clamor coming from the couch, and Joey rolled her eyes when she saw that Colton had spilled, like, half the popcorn on the carpet, and the other half on Aubrey's lap. He was down on the ground trying to pick up all the kernels.

She looked back over at Layla, about to comment on how much of a mess Colton was, but Layla wasn't paying attention to Colton at all. She was still looking at Joey. "What did you want to ask me?" Joey said, whispering, realizing just how close Layla was.

Layla pulled on her hoodie string before saying, "I never asked . . . But you and me, we started working on our project, and the 23andMe stuff, and we were just friends again. But you never told me why you stopped being my friend in the first place. Did I do something?"

Joey hadn't considered that Layla might think it was her fault. It was the opposite of Layla's fault. But how on earth was Joey supposed to explain? How could Joey tell her that she didn't want to hurt Layla, that she had *feelings* for Layla? She couldn't have this conversation here, in the back of Jackson's living room, with all her teammates and brothers sitting just a few feet away.

"You didn't do anything," Joey said. "Can we just forget it?"

Layla frowned. "No."

Joey shifted away from Layla. She couldn't do this with Layla's vanilla smell all in her nose. "Just watch the movie, Layla."

She leaned against the wall, eyes forward, and swallowed hard. Layla fell quiet, too, and Joey braced herself for Layla to go sit with Colton. But she didn't move.

They watched the movie. Or, at least pretended to, for a while, until Joey couldn't help but say, "I got scared."

Layla answered immediately. "Of what?"

"Of how I am. And . . ." Joey had to force the words out. "And how I feel about you."

Layla moved closer, so that they were touching thigh to thigh again. "What do you mean?" Layla asked, and it was too much. Her voice was too soft, her leg felt too good against Joey's. Layla was looking at Joey like she had all the patience in the world, and no one else in her life had any patience for her lately.

Layla was tugging on her hoodie string and Joey reached to pull it out of Layla's hand, accidentally pulling Layla closer with it.

Joey, without thinking, kissed her.

And then immediately realized what she was doing, and pushed away, bumping hard against the wall, leaning back and putting as much space as she could between them. "Layla, I . . . I didn't mean to . . . I'm . . ." Joey's chest squeezed tight and she started breathing a little too quickly.

"Okay, wait," Layla said. "Joey, don't—"

Joey was scrambling to her feet and wasn't exactly quiet about it. Someone from the couch in front of them, Joey didn't even know who, said, "What are you two even doing back there?"

Joey felt like suddenly everyone was looking at her instead of the movie, and Joey knew the feeling that was in her chest right now, she knew that everything was going to grow tighter and tighter until she screamed or hit or ruined another party. She looked at Layla, who was still sitting on the floor, and Joey couldn't be near her anymore, she couldn't. Not with these feelings swirling inside of her and making her feel like her lungs were going to explode.

Layla started to stand, but Joey quickly shook her head, backing away from her. "I just need . . . don't follow me, Layla, just . . . *don't*."

Joey rushed out of the living room, out of the front door and into the fresh, cold November air. It hit her face, and felt good, because Joey was hot, Joey was sweating, Joey could not seem to catch her breath no matter how hard she was trying to breathe. She sat down on the curb in front of Jackson's house, putting her head between her knees.

She fumbled for her phone in her pocket and pulled it out to . . . to what? Call Mom? *Mom, I can't breathe, come get me.*

Joey's vision went blurry with tears as she looked at her Mom's contact in her phone. She couldn't call her. Mom would assume Joey did something; she would assume that the party somehow got ruined because Joey was *Joey*. She didn't want to hear the disappointment in her mom's voice when she picked up the phone.

She didn't want to have to say, *I didn't do anything but I need you, please don't be mad at me.*

Joey heard the front door open, and she knew what would happen next. It would be Jackson's parents, or Layla, or even Jackson, and someone would say something, and Joey would do something *Joey* and then someone else would be calling Mom, anyway, and Joey would get in trouble and everyone would be mad, and, and, and . . .

"Joey? What's going on?"

It was Colton's voice.

Joey lifted her head. Colton was standing next to her. A little behind them, Thomas stood near the front door. Colton was handing Joey her jacket. She took it from him, wrapping it around her shoulders. She hadn't realized she was shivering.

"What happened?" Thomas asked.

Joey bit the inside of her cheek hard. She wouldn't cry in front of her brothers. She wouldn't yell at them, either. "I messed up. *Again.*"

Colton took a seat next to Joey on the ground. "But what did you do? Layla just said you wanted space, but she looked kind of weird. I told you not to hurt—"

"I kissed her," Joey interrupted.

Which shut Colton right up. "Oh."

"You kissed *Layla*?" Thomas asked, his voice high. "Did she get mad?"

Joey didn't respond. Her cheeks were hot, and she didn't want to explain any of this to her brothers, of all people. She buried her face back into her knees.

"Do you want to go home?" Colton asked.

Thomas came over to sit beside him.

Joey shook her head. "I didn't want Mom to think . . ."

"I'll call," Colton said. "We can just tell her we're ready to go home. Okay, Thomas?"

Thomas shrugged. "The movie was boring anyway, I guess."

Colton called Mom, and Layla never came outside to join them. The three of them sat together on Jackson's front stoop until Mom's car pulled around the corner. No one said much of anything on the drive home, but no one accused Joey of ruining their night, either.

There was a moment though—a very real moment after Joey kissed Layla, and everyone turned to look at them, and everything felt like too much—that Joey thought she might push Layla. She thought she might even hit her.

Maybe her brothers weren't accusing her of anything, but Joey, at the very least, ruined her own night.

And probably her friendship with Layla, for good this time.

19

The last thing Joey wanted to do was celebrate Thanksgiving. As if she had anything to be thankful for. As if anyone was actually thankful to be stuck with her, either.

Every year, Thanksgiving was a little different, but mostly the same. Sometimes Joey's grandparents came, sometimes Luka had a girlfriend to bring. Once, Benny didn't come because he was doing some ridiculous Friendsgiving thing instead. This year, it would be just the triplets, their moms, Luka, and Benny. Which, even though she was dreading celebrating, Joey thought was perfect.

She was glad Luka wasn't dating anyone. It wasn't that she didn't want Luka to be happy and have a girl-friend, it was just that it meant Joey wouldn't have to feel uncomfortable the entire time with some woman she didn't know making small talk with everyone.

This year, Joey was really glad there weren't going to be any strangers at their Thanksgiving. She couldn't deal with anyone new. She couldn't even deal with her grandparents. If they weren't already well aware of who Joey was lately, she didn't want to deal with it. She just wanted to enjoy Benny being there, and hoped every-thing could almost feel normal.

All three of Joey's brothers were happy to have a long weekend. Joey, who hadn't been in school for two weeks, would finally be going back come Monday. She was sitting at the kitchen counter with Benny, who was pulling up his midterm grades to show Mom, while Mama had the three of them stuffing mushrooms. Mama had a turkey in the oven, but had—grudgingly, and after much begging from Luka—allowed Luka, Colton, and Thomas to deep-fry another turkey outside.

(Joey was outside with them at first, but Colton started FaceTiming with Layla, and Joey didn't want to hear Layla's voice. She was doing a really good job of avoiding her. Again.)

They didn't exactly need two turkeys, and her moms weren't confident it would turn out okay—especially when Mom found Colton reading an article on his phone titled "How to Deep-Fry a Turkey without Killing Yourself."

"Once you pull those grades up, I'm sending you outside to supervise your father and brothers," Mom said. Benny tapped a link and then handed over his phone. "Look at you! These are awesome. I'm so proud of you, babe."

Benny blushed as Mom pulled him in for a hug. "I know you miss me, and I miss you, too, seriously. But as you can see, I'm doing good at Dad's."

Mama glanced at Mom from where she was standing at the stove before saying to Benny, "It's not the same without you, but we're glad you're happy."

"Maybe you can spend Christmas break here with us, though?" Mom added. "Since, you know. No school to focus on."

Joey held her breath until Benny answered, "Yeah, I guess that'd be cool. I cannot wait, for the record. I need a break from school so bad."

"Speaking of breaks from school!" Mom said, pulling out her own phone. "I should shoot an email to Joey's teachers to see if there's anything she needs to do before they get her back on Monday. Becca, what's the password for the school email?"

"It's Thanksgiving," Mama said.

"The password?"

"No, I mean, don't email them on Thanksgiving, they're probably with their families," Mama corrected.

Mom licked the mushroom stuffing off her fingers. "I want to give them time to respond before the weekend's over. What's the password?"

Mama wiped her hand on the dish towel before reaching down to pull out a pot from the cabinet to fill with water. "The triplets' initials and birth year."

"That's not exactly secure," Benny commented, as he got up to wash the mushroom gunk off his hands.

"Who's hacking into a school account to send emails? We barely use this as it is. I think we've sent a total of three emails since the kids started at that school," Mom said.

Benny flicked his wet hands at Joey, little splashes at her face, and she laughed and pushed him away from her. She was about to ask Mama how long the mushrooms would take to cook, because stuffing them was making Joey want to eat them now, when Mom asked Mama, "Hon, were you writing an email . . ." before her voice trailed off.

Joey suddenly realized two things.

One, she forgot all about the saved email drafts that she never sent to any of the 23andMe connections.

And two, her mom was *right now* reading them.

"Mom, wait," Joey said, as her mom stood up.

"Something wrong?" Mama asked, noticing the serious look on Mom's face, the way Mom was squinting, focused, on her cell phone. "What is it?"

Mom looked like she forgot she was in a kitchen full of other people. She glanced at Joey, then at Mama, and back again, before shaking her head and looking back down at the phone. "Nothing, um. I'll be right back? I just need to go upstairs for a minute."

Mama looked concerned. "You okay?"

Mom's smile was tight as she nodded. "I'm fine, yeah. I just think I'm getting a headache, and I'm gonna go take something quick."

"You can lay down for a bit if you need," Mama said, walking over to Mom, wrapping her arm around her waist and kissing her on the cheek. Mom didn't return the embrace. She was halfway out the kitchen already. "Joey and I can handle things in here."

Mom looked at Joey again, hesitating. Joey wondered if she was waiting for Joey to say something, to explain.

But Mom turned and left the kitchen, and Joey sat there, the stuffed mushrooms in front of her, wondering if she was supposed to try and follow Mom.

She didn't.

20

Joey didn't know what to do. She wanted to text Layla, but she couldn't. She wanted to pull Colton aside and tell him what happened, but she didn't want to make him feel bad, or make him mad at her all over again, either. She wanted to keep pretending like Mom hadn't seen Joey's email drafts, to just continue with Thanksgiving as normal, but she knew she wouldn't be able to pretend forever.

Or could she? It wasn't like Mom yelled at Joey. She hadn't said anything. She stayed upstairs for about a half hour before coming back down, kissing Mama, and going outside to supervise the boys.

Maybe she didn't see the unsent emails? Maybe it *was* just a headache?

But when Joey pulled out her phone and logged in to the school email account, all those email drafts had been deleted.

"Jo! Come on, we're gonna get the game started," Benny said, sticking his head into the kitchen. "You're with Mom and me as usual."

They played a game of football together every year. Joey was almost always on a team with Mom and Benny. They let Mama and Luka be on the same team with Colton and Thomas because Mama was hopelessly awful, and it made the teams feel pretty even. Joey, though she never really cared about football, usually loved this. Colton got really competitive, and so did Benny and Mom. Thomas and Mama didn't usually do all that much, so Luka (with some help from Colton) basically carried the team. Last year, Joey scored the very first touchdown, and Benny ran around the backyard with her on his shoulders, cheering.

"Mom's playing?" Joey asked. "I mean, she doesn't have a headache or whatever?"

"She's good to go. Let's do this!" Benny said, holding his hand out for her to take.

Joey thought about that hand, the DNA that created it. Joey was the only one on their team who wasn't biologically related to them, and she wondered if Benny wished his dad was on his team instead of her, so it would be Mom's DNA versus Mama's DNA. Joey wondered what the donor was doing right now, if he had a family that he was playing football with, if he was celebrating Thanksgiving with a big meal, too.

Thinking about that made her stomach hurt.

"I think I'll sit this out," Joey said.

"No way. It's a tradition! We need you, Joey!"

Outside, Colton had the football at the center of the small backyard. Joey followed Benny across the concrete deck. Since they'd only lived there for about a month, they'd never played here before, so Colton and Luka were deciding what would count as part of the field and what would count as the end zones.

Joey followed Benny over to Mom, and she was surprised when Mom wrapped an arm around Joey, pulling her into a side hug before shouting, "You guys are going down!"

Joey glanced up at her, but Mom wouldn't meet her gaze.

"Huddle up!" Luka called to his team, and as they all gathered, Joey felt herself dragged close by Benny.

It made her feel a little suffocated.

But as soon as the huddle was done, she was able to get a little space, especially since their play was almost always for Joey to go long. Benny and Mom could throw really well, and Joey was fast and could catch. Thomas was fast, too—he was the best at stealing the bases during baseball season—so the other team would normally have him block Joey.

Colton was blocking her this year, though. He wasn't as fast, but he was better at it, so Joey had a hard time getting open. It was frustrating, especially since he kept grabbing at her shirt or her pants, which was against the rules.

She shoved her elbow into his chest.

"*Oof,*" Colton said, doubling over a bit.

"Joey, *watch it,*" Mom snapped in warning. "I will make you sit out, you understand me?"

It distracted Joey enough for Colton to intercept the ball as Benny tried to pass it to her, and he took off running, throwing it to Luka, who dodged past Mom and scored a touchdown. Their team all ran in for a hug, and Benny took the ball from his dad.

"Shake it off, Jo!" Benny said, and she tried. She tried to remember how much she usually loved this.

Luckily, Joey's team started scoring touchdowns, which made Colton mad, and she stuck her tongue out at him. Luka and Mom started bickering as usual over whether or not his throw was in bounds, and whether or not an interception was an interception, and whether or not a touchdown was a touchdown, and, well, everything.

Thomas laughed his donkey laugh along with Mama, while Mama mostly kept to some corner of the field, out of the way, as she watched everyone else play.

Luka, just like in gym class, didn't let Mama get away with that for long, though. "Becca, head in the game! I'm getting this one to you, you're gonna get us our big win!" he said. As it was, their team was down by only a touchdown.

"Not getting anything past me!" Mom said, wrapping her arms around Mama's waist. "Not while I'm guarding this one."

"Boys, go get your mom out of the way for us, will you?" Luka said, which sent Thomas and Colton running over to Mom, basically yanking her away from Mama. Which was against the rules and had Joey scowling. Apparently *they* were allowed to break the rules, but the second that Joey elbowed Colton, *she* was immediately yelled at.

"That's cheating!" Joey yelled. "Get off her!"

"We're gonna win, just like we *always* do, Joey! Face it!" Colton yelled.

"Because you always cheat!" Joey yelled back, annoyed.

She watched as Benny ran over and grabbed both Colton and Thomas. "That's right! Look at these little cheaters!" Benny was saying. The four of them—Mom, Benny, Thomas, and Colton—fell to the ground, a tangled, piled mess.

Luka seized the moment. "Becca, catch!"

"You can't throw it!" Joey shouted. None of this should count. They should be calling a time out at the very least. This wasn't fun; Joey was getting mad. "They're all on the ground, there's no tackling!"

"Ignore her, Becca, catch!"

Luka threw the ball. Joey watched it spiral toward

Mama. If the other team could cheat, so could she. If they could tackle, *so could she*. She took off running toward Mama, as fast as she could. The ball was a little faster, and Mama had her hands in the air to catch it. Only, Mama was awful at football, so she missed, and the ball sailed over her head.

Joey couldn't stop her momentum though. Just as the ball went over Mama's head, Joey threw her entire weight at Mama's middle, wrapping her arms tightly around her, and tackling her hard to the grass.

Mama's head hit the ground first.

Everything stood still for a moment as Joey lay on top of Mama, who didn't move right away. But then everything sped up as Mama brought a hand to her head and suddenly Joey was getting yanked off of her—roughly—as Mom came over and pushed her off. "Becca? Becca, are you okay?" Mom's voice sounded far away in Joey's ears.

She reached behind Mama to feel her head and pulled away with some blood on her hand. Joey stared at that blood. It was *so red*. Mama's eyes opened but they didn't look right, like she just woke up from sleeping, all groggy, as she blinked up at Mom. "I just hit the ground wrong," Mama was saying.

And then Mom turned to Joey. "What is *wrong* with you! What the *hell* is wrong with you!"

"I didn't mean . . ."

"Mom, is she okay?" Benny asked, Luka right behind him.

"I don't know, I can't . . . Becca, sweetheart, turn your head. Let me see."

Mom sounded frantic, and Joey couldn't breathe. *She did this.*

She did this, and she couldn't breathe, she couldn't breathe.

The next thing Joey knew, she was backing away from them, backing away from her family as they surrounded her mama, before she turned around and started running. She ran as fast as she could, needing to not be there, not be anywhere near Mom, or Mama, or any of them.

Joey didn't even think they noticed she left. She didn't think any of them cared she was gone, anyway.

21

Joey walked, without her jacket, shivering, along the familiar path without thinking about where she was going or what she would do when she got there. She didn't care. She just kept hearing those sounds: the one Mama's head made when it bounced against the ground, and the one in Mom's voice as she pushed Joey away.

Being mean to Thomas was bad. Getting them kicked out of the apartment, and making Benny want to move out, was awful.

This, Joey knew, was unforgivable.

This was what Joey was afraid of, and she didn't

know if Mama was okay (would Mama be okay?) and she didn't know if Mom could ever love her after this.

Joey stood in front of the entrance to Mama's favorite Hartshorne Park trail. She glanced up at the hill. The trees were blowing in the wind, and Joey tucked her hands in her sweatshirt pocket, trying to find warmth. She hesitated.

Even if Mama was okay . . . would she ever want to walk with Joey again?

Joey closed her eyes, tightly. She didn't want to think about Mama. She didn't want to think about that sound, about the blood from the scrape on the back of her head, about that glassy look in her eyes.

Joey started walking up the trail. She suddenly needed to scream harder than she'd ever needed to scream before, and the top of that hill was the only place she knew she could do that.

She felt her phone buzz and pulled it out of her pocket. She had a missed call from Benny, a text from Colton that said, where are you? moms freaking, and another from Layla that said, Colton called me looking for you is everything ok??

It was too much. Joey's finger hovered over Layla's

name, debating if she should just text Layla and say *I'm fine and I'm sorry and I'm out of the way.*

But she also wanted to text Colton and say *is Mama okay how bad did I hurt her?*

How bad *did* she hurt her?

Joey was having trouble breathing. She was practically running up the trail, and she was panting, breathing heavily through her nose as she climbed. She reached the top of that trail, the view that Mama loved so much, that Mama loved sharing with Joey, that Mama always stood looking at, with her arm around Joey's shoulders, holding her close and tight.

Joey had spent all this time worried about Mom not loving Joey anymore, she had never thought she could do something to make Mama leave her, too. But she *hurt* her. Joey hurt Mama, and kids just didn't do that to their moms. Joey had no answer for why she always caused things like this to happen, she didn't know why she felt this way—and she couldn't fix it and she couldn't go home and she didn't know what to do.

But thinking about biology, about the genes she shared with Mama and not Mom, reminded her of the donor and his family. His biology. Of the

23andMe account full of connections Joey could reach out to.

He could have answers. He could know what to do.

He could maybe, just maybe, even come and get her.

She looked out at that view in front of her. At the waves crashing against the rocks, and the shadows that the clouds made as they blew by overhead. She couldn't see many people below her in town, on the beach. Everyone was home with their families, she figured. It was Thanksgiving, after all.

Joey pulled up the 23andMe account on her phone. She scrolled through and picked a random person—a random person she was related to, she shared DNA with—and clicked on their name. Theresa Page. Joey didn't know who she was, just that she wasn't related to Mama.

All Joey had to do was reach out to her. All Joey had to do was connect with her and write a message saying, *My name is Joey Sennett-Cooper but I might be a Page, too, like you, and I need to know if you get really, really mad ever, or if you know who in your family does. If you know who I am a part of, if you can tell me who I am.*

Joey's fingers hovered over her phone. It would be so easy.

But what would Theresa Page say? Was she home with her family, and would she get the alert and feel . . . happy? Annoyed? None of the people on the donor's side of the family knew Joey and her brothers existed before she made this account, but did they know now? Could they look her up, like she looked them up? Could they find her?

Did she want them to?

No, she thought, her chest tight. No, she didn't want them. She didn't *know* them.

Joey couldn't do this. She couldn't talk to this woman, this random woman she didn't know, even though they shared DNA. The donor didn't know her, either. *She* didn't know *him*. He didn't have her mama's smile and warm cuddles, he didn't know her well enough to refer to her by a little silly nickname like Mom did.

Maybe he knew why she got so angry, maybe he got so angry, too, but he wouldn't know anything else about her.

And Joey didn't want him to.

She didn't want him to. What if someone contacted

her now? What if, now that she had made this account, they tried to reach out to her or Colton or Thomas—and what would that mean? What would happen? *What did she do?* She didn't want this . . . she just wanted to know *why* she got so mad. She didn't want to hurt her family. She didn't want anyone else except for her family.

She needed to delete the account. She needed to figure out how to delete the account, but the settings were confusing and her eyes filled with tears and it was too hard to see the screen, and she didn't know how to do it.

Joey was clenching her teeth so tight her jaw was starting to hurt, and it was hard to breathe, her chest and throat were too tight, and all the familiar feelings swirled around her, making Joey feel like she was going to break into a million pieces if she didn't do something soon. She threw her phone as hard as she possibly could, off that hill, down, down, down toward the rocks and the water and everything below them.

She watched it hit and break and fall.

It wasn't enough.

She needed to scream. She needed to scream and

shout and hit, and she inhaled the crisp air that burned as it filled up her lungs, and—

"*Joey!*"

Joey whimpered as she exhaled, turning around in surprise at the sound of Mom's voice. Mom was standing right there, her hair windblown, her chest heaving as if she had been running. It didn't seem real, and it took Joey a second to get her voice to work. "How?"

Mom took another step forward, trying to catch her breath. "We didn't know where you went, and we used that Find My Phone thing and Mama recognized this place, so she sent me here, and I can't believe you'd—"

Joey's chest squeezed. "Mama's okay?"

"Yes, she's okay. Benny and Luka took her to the hospital to see if she needs stitches. But she's okay," Mom said. She looked scared. "Come away from the edge, Joey. What are you doing?"

"I get so mad sometimes," Joey said. "Mama takes me on these stupid walks, and I can't even . . . I look out and I just want to . . ."

"Want to *what*?" Mom's voice was as frantic as it had been earlier, and it made Joey close her eyes tightly, made her entire body feel tight and tense and awful.

"Scream," Joey admitted, barely above a whisper. "Every time we come, I just want to . . . I *need* to . . ."

Mom came closer, standing right in front of her. Joey wanted her to reach for her and hold her closely. Instead, Mom said, "Then scream."

"What?" Joey asked.

"You need to scream, Joey, then scream." Mom looked out at the view, and Joey wondered for a second if she saw what Mama did. If she could find peace in it, too.

But then Mom started screaming.

Loud, and as hard as she could, with her eyes closed tightly, directed out at that view, out over the rocks and the waves and the water. When she stopped, it echoed. Joey watched, wide-eyed, as Mom took another deep breath, and screamed again.

Joey turned, facing forward, and started screaming, too.

They stood there, shouting side by side, Joey screaming until the air was completely out of her lungs, then taking another deep breath in, letting it fill her up, about to scream again . . . only, she couldn't. The scream, this time, came out as a sob, and Joey covered her face as the tears began spilling, and she started crying and couldn't stop.

Mom's arms suddenly came around Joey's waist, pulling her close, down to the well-worn path and into her lap. "I'm sorry, I'm sorry," Mom was saying, over and over in Joey's ear. "Mama's okay, you're okay."

"No I'm not, I'm *not*," Joey cried.

"You *are* okay, Joey," Mom said. "I've got you, I'm sorry."

"I hurt Mama, I hurt *everyone*." Joey wrapped her arms around Mom, gripping Mom's shirt in her hands, not wanting to let go, not wanting to *ever* let go. "I made Benny leave. I'm sorry, I'm sorry, Mom, don't leave me, please don't go."

"I'm not going anywhere, ever," Mom said. "*Ever*, you hear me?"

Joey cried harder, and Mom continued to hold her, on the ground, in the cold. Joey didn't know how long they stayed that way, how long she kept her face pulled into her mom's plaid top, before she was able to breathe again. She pulled away, wiping at her face, but Mom didn't let her go. "I feel like I've failed you," Mom said.

Joey didn't understand. "How?"

"I've spent all this time . . . yelling, and grounding you, and blaming you." Mom shook her head. "All the while you needed me to see that you needed more than that. All of this is more than just . . . a bad temper, and I know you're a sweet, kind, loving girl, Joey. I'm your mother, I'm supposed to keep you safe."

"You need to keep Mama safe," Joey said.

"I do, yes," Mom agreed. "I need to keep my whole family safe. But not *from you*, Joey. What I really need is to admit when I don't know everything. And I should have given therapy a better try. I don't understand this anger you have, my Little Growl, but I want to."

Joey wanted to feel better . . . but hearing Mom say she didn't understand made Joey think about all of the reasons why she didn't. And all of the reasons she and Layla searched for the donor in the first place.

"Talk to me, Joey," Mom said. "I can see you're lost in thought about something. Your mama gets that same look."

Joey swallowed. "I know you saw those emails and . . . I was only looking for the donor because I thought, maybe, he'd . . ." Joey stopped talking, her voice trailing off as she looked at the way her mom looked down, blinking back tears that had suddenly filled her eyes.

"I just wanted to fix everything," Joey tried to explain.

Mom tried to offer Joey a smile, but it was wobbly as she wiped away a tear. She stood, wiping the dirt off her jeans. "We're going to figure that out together. All of us, me, you, Mama. Your brothers, too."

She held out her hand for Joey to take.

Joey wanted to trust it. She wanted to take Mom's hand, and go home, and go to therapy, and have things work and be fixed and okay. Just like Mom said she wanted.

But there was still so much they didn't understand. Joey still almost really, really hurt Mama today.

"Come on," Mom said, her arm still outstretched. "Let's go wait for Mama at home."

Joey, even though her entire body was still fighting against it, took her hand and let Mom lead her home.

22

When Joey and Mom walked through the door, Thomas and Colton immediately looked up from the TV and asked about a million questions, but Mom sent Joey upstairs to take a shower. Joey was shivering and dirty. A shower sounded good.

Benny and Luka were still with Mama at the hospital, and Mom said she'd call and find out more. Joey stepped under the showerhead and let the hot water hit her. Everything ached. Her chest, her legs, her shoulders. She stayed in that shower longer than she normally would, just trying to feel better.

In her bedroom, she opted to just put on pajamas. She started looking for her cell phone before remembering she threw it down the Hartshorne Park hill. Yet another thing she'd have to confess to her moms, another rash decision she had made.

"I heard you went to our spot without me."

Joey whipped around to see Mama standing in the doorway, leaning against the frame. Her hair was messy and pulled back, and Joey could see the white edges of a bandage poking out from the back, but she smiled at Joey like she hadn't just gotten home from the hospital, like it was just a normal Thanksgiving evening.

Her eyes looked tired, but clear, and Joey's nose burned as she tried her best not to start crying again. She had to stop herself from running right into Mama's arms.

"I could really use a hug," Mama said.

"I don't want to hurt you," Joey said.

Mama crossed the room. "Come here," she said, pulling Joey to her. Joey was afraid to hug Mama too hard, and she was afraid to go near the cut on Mama's head. Still, in Mama's arms, Joey could breathe. She listened to Mama's heartbeat against her ear, wanting to crawl into this feeling and never let it go.

~~~~~•

The next morning, Mom called a family meeting. Joey sat by herself on the love seat, Thomas and Colton were together on the sofa. Benny leaned against the doorway between the living room and kitchen. Mama sat on the edge of the coffee table, Mom sturdy behind her.

"We've got a lot to talk about, Jo-Jo," Mama said to her. "Least of all you running off yesterday and scaring us half to death. But I love you, we both do. And nothing you could do could change that."

Joey shook her head. "But I *heard* you. You told Mom you were scared of me. And you should be. Thomas and Colton and Layla, too. Everybody."

"Joey . . ." Mama sighed.

"We are scared." It was Mom who said it. "Just . . . of all of it. Of how badly you're hurting. Of how incredibly useless we feel."

"Listen to me," Mama said. "We're going to figure this out. I promise you that. We need you to be honest with us, though. Mom told me about the email, about the . . ." She drifted off, glancing over at Colton and Thomas.

"Thomas and Colton know," Joey admitted. "That I was looking for the, uh, donor."

"Wait, the what?" Benny said. He glanced over at Mom, and Joey did, too, but she was looking down at her hands, folded in her lap.

"We told her not to do anything," Colton said.

"Like, the sperm donor?" Benny asked, his voice high.

"Point is, Joey," Mama interrupted, "you went behind our backs, knowing that we've always been open to discussing all of that with you. With all of you. What were you even . . . ?"

"They stole my saliva, by the way," Colton ratted out. "Which, you know. Rude."

"You what?" Mama asked.

Joey shot him a look. "Layla and me, we did 23andMe. Like Layla does with her mom. A bunch of people not related to Mama came up, which means they're, you know, related just to . . . us." Joey glanced over at Mom, who got very quiet.

Benny let out a laugh. "23andMe? The ancestry thing? Jesus, kids these days are way more resourceful than I was at that age."

Mama took a deep breath through her nose, centering herself. "Okay. What you and Layla did was incredibly dangerous, do you understand that? You don't know who you might have . . . We don't know these people. And that account gives them access to you, Joey, which is unsafe."

"But Layla—" Joey started, but Mama interrupted her.

"Has parental supervision. Her mom is in charge of their account, not Layla. But there *are* resources available to you. Options. If *any* of you are curious, you need to come to us." Mama paused, rolling her shoulders and closing her eyes for a moment.

"Are you okay?" Thomas asked.

"Just a headache," Mama said.

"Which brings us to our next topic," Mom said, jumping in. "Mama and I are committed to making sure that Joey gets the help she needs. We've dropped the ball on that."

Thomas looked confused. "Get Joey help with what?"

"Listen, babe, I know it's not easy to understand, but we think that Joey cannot always control herself. It doesn't make the way she sometimes treats you or her friends right. But she deserves to be happy, too, yeah?" Mom smiled at him. "If we get her the help she needs, we're hoping everyone can be a little happier."

"You know how I take medication for my ADHD?" Benny asked Thomas, who nodded. "Maybe there's something like that for Joey. Without my meds, I was jumpy and a little out of control, too. I couldn't help it."

Mama smiled at Benny. "Thank you. Now, boys, if you have any other questions, we're happy to answer them," Mama said. "But we'd really like some time alone with your sister, if that's okay."

Benny motioned for Colton and Thomas. "Let's go play video games or something."

Thomas got up off the couch. He glanced warily at Joey, as if he wanted to believe Benny and their moms, but wasn't sure. Joey didn't blame him. She still wasn't entirely convinced that going to doctors or therapists was going to magically make it easy to be nicer.

Colton hovered for a minute. He made eye contact

with Joey, who looked away quickly. "You should tell them about Eli."

"About who now?" Mom asked, sounding exhausted.

It made Joey blush.

"Layla yelled at me the other day, because she says he bullies Joey," Colton said.

"Colton, shut up," Joey said.

"*Hey,*" Mom said.

"I didn't think about it, or stop it, or whatever, which is why Layla was mad," Colton said. He stared at Joey for a moment, waiting for her to say something.

She scowled.

"Fine, I'll tell them then," Colton said. "Mom, he shoves her all the time. Like, slams her into walls, and calls her names. He's the one who started calling her Bruiser, you know."

"You all call me *Growl!* It's the same thing!"

"No it's not!" Colton continued. "He slapped her across the face with a piece of pizza."

"He did *what?*" Mom snapped.

"This is none of your business, Colton!" Joey shouted.

"Okay, Colton, go with your brothers," Mama said.

"Joey, take a deep breath, okay? Can you do that for me?"

Joey hung her head as Colton left the room. The last thing she wanted to do was start a fight, get mad and yell and throw things.

"Tell us about Eli," Mom said. "He's on the hockey team, right? I can call Luka. I *will* call Luka. No one is allowed to put their hands on you, or call you names, or treat you like—"

"Like I treat everyone?" Joey scoffed.

"Hey," Mama said, raising her voice for the first time that morning. She got up off the coffee table and crossed to sit close to Joey on the love seat. "You listen to me, okay? Your anger does *not* make you disposable. It does not make your safety and well-being any less of a priority. You understand me? I have heard so much self-loathing from you these past couple of days and it hurts my heart, Jo-Jo."

"Your mama's right," Mom said. "We love you. We're here for you."

Joey shook her head, the familiar feeling that she hated, *she hated so much*, swelling up in her gut. "You can walk away!"

"Excuse me?" Mom said.

"You and Benny could just walk away! It's why Benny moved out, because he can, and you can, because we're half Mama and half the donor and none of you . . . you don't have to . . . you could just leave if you wanted and nothing matters and . . ." Joey stopped talking, trying to breathe, trying to keep the tears at bay.

But when she looked up, she realized Mom wasn't as successful. "Joey, I . . ." It was all Mom got out before she buried her face in her hands, crying.

Joey couldn't remember the last time she saw Mom cry like this. If ever.

"Joey," Mama said, rubbing Joey's back and looking over at Mom. Her mouth moved without saying anything for a moment, like she was trying to figure out what to say. "Is that what your outburst in class was about? Is that what this is about? You know that love makes a family. That biology does not. We've talked about this so much. Your mother loves you so much, and she is *one hundred percent* your mother."

"No, I know, that's not what I—"

"You think I could just walk away?" Mom interrupted. Her voice was wobbly, her cheeks stained with tears. "You think I could ever just . . . I could *never* just . . . You are a part of me, Joey. You are the best part of me. I know we're different, *I'm* different, and it can be confusing, and weird, maybe, sometimes, but the one thing that makes the most sense to me is how much I need you and your brothers in my life."

Mom stopped, pausing to take a deep breath, to wipe her face. She looked over at Mama, who nodded her head. "Talk to her, Steph," Mama said.

"It hurts, okay?" Mom admitted. "It *hurt* when I saw those emails, and that you looked up the donor searching for answers that I wish that I could give you. *I* want to give you everything."

Joey was crying now, too. "You were just always so mad at me."

Mom was across the room, pulling Joey into her. "I'm sorry if you thought, even for a second, that my being angry with you made me love you any less, or that Benny moving out had anything to do with how he feels about our family. We have a lot to figure out, Little Growl. But I promise you that we will figure all of this out."

Joey cried into Mom's shirt, again, and Mama

wrapped her arms around the both of them, a full mom-sandwich, all three of them in tears.

Joey wasn't convinced that everything was okay.

But it felt good to have both of her mothers holding her close instead of pushing her away.

23

"**I'm glad you decided to come back, Joey,**" **Dr.** Collins said. "I know it's not easy for you to be here."

Joey sat in Dr. Collins's office, leaning up against the arm of the couch. She didn't want to sit between her moms this time, so she immediately sat as close to the edge of the couch as she could, trying to find safety in that small room. Her moms were sitting close together, Mama holding tightly to Mom's hand. Mom's leg was bouncing a bit like Joey's sometimes did.

"I just want to remind you that this is a safe place. Your moms and I are here to listen, not to judge or get you in trouble," Dr. Collins said. "I say this because you don't look like you feel all that comfortable right now."

Joey squirmed a little bit. She wanted to be here. Well, no, that wasn't true. She didn't want to be here at all, doing this. But it made Mama look so happy when Joey agreed to try again, and Joey did want to fix all of this, she *did*. If being here was part of that, then she had no real choice, did she?

"I think that's my fault," Mom suddenly spoke up, which took Joey by surprise. Mom was looking down, gripping Mama's hand in her lap. "I wasn't exactly open to all of this, which Joey knows. And I guess I didn't understand that something was actually wrong, so I kept pushing Joey away. I didn't know how to deal with all of this, and I let my own feelings get in the way. So, um. I guess I just wanted to apologize. To you, Dr. Collins, for how I acted the last time we were here. And to Joey."

"How do you feel about that, Joey?" Dr. Collins said.

Joey shrugged.

"Your mom's being vulnerable here. I don't think that's very easy for her. Right? Do you think you can open yourself up and be honest for her, too?" Dr. Collins said.

"It's not easy for either of them," Mama added. "They're both very similar in that way."

Something about the way Mama said that made Joey want to try. "I just . . ." Joey stopped talking. It *was* hard.

"Go ahead," Dr. Collins said.

Joey took a deep breath. "I just don't get how this helps? If something is wrong with me, how is this supposed to do anything? When people get sick or whatever, you do a bunch of tests to figure out what's the problem. Or even like in science class. Mr. Hoover has us start with a hypothesis and then we experiment. That's how you get answers. That's what I was trying to do."

"You mean when you made the 23andMe account, looking for genetic matches?" Dr. Collins asked.

Joey nodded, glancing warily at her moms. "Well, yeah. Mama *never* feels like I do, when I get angry. I thought, maybe, one of them would?"

"And how do you feel, Joey? Can you explain that to me, to your moms?"

Joey didn't know how to explain how she felt to people who had never felt this way, not like her. But then she thought about her and Mom, on the Hartshorne Park hill on Thanksgiving. "Like I have to scream. Like my whole body gets super tight"—Joey made fists and clenched her jaw—"and I can't breathe and I'm gonna just . . . explode, I guess."

"So, then you explode?" Dr. Collins asked.

Joey slowly nodded. "Yeah. But . . . I wanted to find out why. I never know why I can't stop it."

Joey felt a hand on her thigh, squeezing gently, and she looked over to see Mom watching her carefully. Both of her moms were.

She carefully glanced back at Dr. Collins. "Do *you* know why?"

"Well, that's what we're here to figure out," Dr. Collins said, smiling at her. "It could be a number of things though, and none of them make you wrong. It'll just mean that your mind works a little differently than other people. Intense anger, especially with children, can stem from anxiety or ADHD—"

"My brother has ADHD," Joey interrupted. "I mean, my older brother. My mom's . . . we don't have any genes in common, but Benny said that before he started taking medicine for it, he had issues, too."

"He did," Mom said. "He'd be bouncing off of the walls. Quick to make rash decisions. Jesus, once he had a school dance to go to, and couldn't decide on what shirt he wanted to wear, and basically destroyed his closet. It was different from this, but . . ."

"But these things affect kids differently," Dr. Collins finished for Mom. "There's also sensory processing issues, where you could get overwhelmed easily by a number of different factors. And there are things like bipolar disorder—"

"That sounds a little intense," Mama admitted.

Dr. Collins nodded. "It can be. And I'm sure it's a lot to hear. But our job right now is two things: One, to understand that there is a perfectly normal explanation for Joey's anger, one that she may not be in control of at all. And two, to figure out what those triggers for that anger are. To talk, openly, about those outbursts. Joey, your parents have a responsibility to make sure that you don't hurt yourself or others, so none of this gives you a free pass. But the more we can learn how to communicate, the easier it'll be to find a diagnosis."

"And then, what?" Joey asked. "I'll take medicine like Benny?"

Dr. Collins shrugged. "You might, yes. For now, we take it one day at a time. We'll set up regular appointments together, with your moms and maybe some with just you and me. Maybe even some with your brothers. I'll teach you some coping strategies for when you start feeling that tightness in your body, that need to scream. Together, we'll see if we can find the ones that work best for you. That's our priority to start."

Joey looked back over at her moms. She wanted to know what they were thinking. She wanted to know if they thought this was fixable. If Mom thought this would help.

"What if it takes too long," Joey found herself saying. "What if Benny never wants to come home because I don't get better fast enough. Or I hurt Colton, or Thomas, or Mama again. What if Mom—"

"I'm not leaving," Mom interrupted. "Nothing you can do can make me not want you. You hear me? *Nothing.* And you are not the reason Benny has been staying with his dad."

Mama chimed in, explaining for Dr. Collins, "When we moved into the motel, it was just too cramped, and Benny has a room at his dad's house. He chose to stay there more often, because it's been good for him, for his schoolwork. It can be crazy in our house on a good day, and with his ADHD and the stress of senior year . . . We decided to honor his wishes to stay with his dad for now."

"Not that we're thrilled with it," Mom added, voice low. "But we're just trying to do what's best, I guess."

"What do you think about that, Joey?" Dr. Collins asked.

Joey paused to think about it. She wasn't sure. It didn't change the fact that Benny left because of the motel, which was Joey's fault. It didn't change the fact that she had hurt Mama.

"It's okay if you're not sure how you feel, yet. It's okay to still be hurt and confused," Dr. Collins said. "We aren't going to solve everything in one session. Just like in your science class. You don't start with the answers, right? You start with the hypothesis. It takes time from there."

"Well, okay," Joey said. "Then what's our hypothesis?"

"What do you think it should be?" Dr. Collins asked back.

Joey shook her head. "I don't know. I guess . . . 'Joey is sometimes mean and bad because she's all messed up and if we keep coming to therapy maybe we'll fix her so she's not messed up anymore'?"

"No," Mom said, her voice strong. "More like . . . Joey acts out because we haven't figured out the root of the problem yet, but once we do, and we work at it together, she'll be okay."

"That sounds like a good one to me," Dr. Collins said. "What do you think, Joey?"

Joey thought about it. *Would* she be okay?

She supposed, like any good science experiment, only time would tell. "Yeah. I think that sounds okay."

When they got home, her brothers were all waiting for them in the living room. Benny had been staying with them all week; it made Joey feel both really happy and really guilty.

"Hi, my baby boys," Mom said as she pulled off her jacket.

Mama kissed Joey on the side of the head before walking past her to head toward the kitchen. "I'll have dinner ready in like a half hour, you all should wash up."

Mom followed her, stopping to grasp Benny's shoulder. She leaned into him, pressing a kiss against the side of his head as she quietly said, "Spend some time with your sister, okay?"

Not quietly enough, of course, because everyone else heard her just fine. Joey really didn't want her family looking at her like she was something to be studied in a petri dish.

Joey sighed as Mom left the room and Benny looked at her. "You don't have to," Joey said. "Mom's just being Mom."

Benny reached out for the sleeve of her shirt, tugging her close and pulling her in for a bear hug. She laughed as she struggled a bit against his tight grip. "Maybe I want to, Jo-Jo," Benny said. "I was gonna stay home tonight anyway. Let's watch a movie or something, okay? You can pick."

Joey felt herself blush under the attention. But still, she smiled at the fact that Benny called this *home*. She hadn't heard him call it that since they moved in. "I don't need to pick the movie," Joey said.

"I'll pick!" Colton chimed in.

"Absolutely not, you have horrible taste," Benny responded.

"I'll pick, then," Thomas said.

The boys carried on, and Joey excused herself to go upstairs. She needed some alone time after talking with Dr. Collins.

She sighed when she realized Colton was following her. "How was it? Your therapist, I mean."

"Fine," she said, hoping to make a beeline for her room and to be done with this conversation. Eventually, her moms said her brothers would come to a therapy session with them. Joey wasn't particularly looking forward to that. It was hard enough talking with her moms there.

"Hey, wait, I wanted to ask," Colton said before Joey could reach her bedroom. "Have you talked to Layla?"

"What? No," Joey said, not expecting him to ask that. She hadn't talked to Layla. Besides when working on their project in class together, they hadn't talked in school this week, hadn't texted. Joey had pretty much avoided even looking in Layla's direction. "Why?"

Colton shot her a look. "Stop being a jerk and just

talk to her. I told her everything that happened at Thanksgiving. Don't look at me like that! I had to, I called her when you went missing so I had to explain. I just think you should just . . . talk to her. I don't think she's mad at you."

Thomas made his way up the stairs, and Colton and Joey fell quiet. He looked back and forth at them as they stood in the middle of the hallway together. "What's going on?" Thomas asked.

"I'm trying to make Joey talk to Layla," Colton said.

"Oh," Thomas said. And then they all just stood there in silence.

Joey looked at them. Her brothers had the same hair, the same eyes, the same nose. The tips of both of their ears turned pink when they felt awkward. They were pink right now, both of them so much alike.

But Joey looked just like them, too. No matter what made them different, they were her brothers, and that mattered. "I'm really trying not to be so mean, Thomas," she said.

He blinked at her for a moment before the blush spread to his cheeks, too, and he looked away. "Yeah, I know. I get it."

But Joey realized that he *didn't* get it. He couldn't, because Joey still didn't get it, either. Dr. Collins said that they were looking for a reason why Joey was the way she was, but that didn't give her a free pass to hurt people, either. Thomas was someone Joey had hurt, over and over again.

"I *am* sorry, Thomas," Joey said. "I know you don't believe me. But I'm trying to figure this out, so I can fix things. Moms are helping, and Dr. Collins is gonna teach me coping strategies or whatever. I don't *want* to hurt you."

"I just don't get why it's always me," Thomas quietly admitted.

Joey didn't know how to answer him. It wasn't just him, but it was *always* him, and that was Joey's fault, not his. She was a bad sister to him. It hurt to think about, but it was true, wasn't it? Why should he even believe that she'd change? She wasn't even sure that *she* believed it.

But . . . they were all actually going to try, right? Her moms were there to help her. They were *going to* help her. Maybe it would all work. Maybe it wouldn't. Dr. Collins couldn't even really answer all of Joey's questions.

"Guys! Dinner will be done in like, ten minutes, someone come set the table!" Mama called from downstairs.

Thomas was still looking at Joey, and she didn't know what else she could say. She didn't know how to make it right yet. She didn't know when she'd be able to. She thought about the things she said to him at the Halloween party, and all of the things she had done and said to him even before that. She thought, again, about the sound of Mama's head hitting the ground.

"I'll keep trying to make it right," Joey said. "I promise."

It was the best that she could do for now. She knew it wasn't exactly enough yet. Joey just had to hope, worry swirling around in her stomach, that she and her brothers would always be okay.

Thomas nodded. "Okay," he said.

It was a start. Joey would take it.

24

Joey sat alone, as usual, tying up her skates for hockey practice. She had finally asked Mom, the night before, to show her how. As she finished up now, they felt nice and tight against her ankles.

Mama had just dropped off her and Colton. Joey wasn't entirely sure what she was still doing here. She wasn't even sure she really liked hockey. Did she? She wasn't Benny; her issues weren't the same as his, and hockey didn't seem to get any of her aggression out like it was supposed to. Not that a decision about hockey mattered right now anyway. Joey knew her moms well. Joey had made a commitment, so they'd want her to at least try to see it through for the rest of the season. Joey could at least do that. It wasn't like she did much more than sit on the bench during games, anyway.

"Hey," Mama had said before Joey could get out of the car. "I just want to give you a heads-up that Mom and I talked to Luka about Eli."

"What? Why?" Joey said. "What did you tell him?"

"Remember what Dr. Collins said, Joey. You deserve to feel safe. A boy putting his hands on you, regardless of anything else, is not safe. And I'd feel better knowing that Luka was keeping an eye out. Okay?" Mama said.

It wasn't like Joey could really argue with her at this point anyway.

She tugged her laces tighter and stood to make her way over to the ice. She hadn't been to practice the entire time she was suspended, and it took her a minute to steady herself.

"Bruiser! You're back!" Eli said the minute Joey stepped onto the ice.

Colton skated up behind him. "Don't call her that," he said.

Joey wished they'd both just leave her alone. She skated away from them, moving quickly around the ice, letting the cold air of the rink hit her face and burn her cheeks the faster she went. She ignored everyone until Luka blew his whistle and called them to the center to start running drills.

Halfway through practice, Luka split them up in pairs. Joey wanted to ask Colton to pair with her, but Eli beat him. "Be with me, Joey," he said, and Colton partnered with Jackson instead. Colton kept glancing Joey's way, and that annoyed Joey, too. He hadn't known anything was wrong until Layla had said something to him, and now he was acting like he had to protect her or something.

Joey didn't need his protection. She was faster than Eli, even if he had better stick control. If she started with the puck, she'd get around him, easy.

But Eli was a puck hog, so of course he said, "I'll start."

He took off toward the net, more powerful than her on his skates, nearly getting past her. She chased after him, catching up to him easily but unable to get around his shoulder. She shoved him a little, out of the line of fire, so that when he did take his shot, he missed.

Joey hurried after the puck. If she could get it, she could score on Eli. She knew she could. All she would have to do was maintain control of the puck. All she had to do was concentrate on that.

She got the puck, skated past Eli, and headed toward her net, when suddenly she felt something jerk her back. Eli had his hand gripped tightly into the collar of her shirt and he yanked it. Joey was losing her balance, she was going to fall, but Eli pushed her into the wall of the rink, hard, took the puck back, and scored.

"You cheated!" Joey yelled, skating back over to him. She shoved him, and he shoved her back.

"Don't be a sore loser, Bruiser," Eli said.

"Hey! Eli and Joey!" Luka yelled, skating over to where they were arguing. "What was that? You think I didn't see that?"

"She's just mad I scored on her," Eli said.

Joey resigned herself for the lecture.

But then Luka said, "You think I didn't see you grab her shirt and throw her into the wall? You think that's okay, Eli? That's not okay, that's not defense, that's not how we play. Not on the ice, not off it. Period. You're on the bench watching for the rest of practice."

"But Coach—" Eli tried to argue.

"Go, Eli. Now."

Eli huffed, but skated off, and Luka turned to focus on Joey. Her cheeks felt warm, and she glanced around the ice at everyone else, who were all clearly watching. "Thanks," she mumbled.

"Listen to me, kid, I saw you run up and shove him, too. You can't do that, either. But I know this has been going on for a while, and I owe you an apology for not noticing. I don't exactly like hearing it from Steph instead of you, though. I'd rather hear it from you, so we can take care of it. You hear me?" Luka said.

Joey nodded her head.

"I know that . . . I know it's kinda strange, that I'm your coach. And Steph said Benny living with me has been hard, too. Just . . . what I'm trying to say is that I'm on your side, okay?"

Joey looked up at him, the sound of skates skidding on ice all around her. He looked so much like Benny, and Joey loved Benny. Luka was just another piece to that puzzle. "Okay."

"Alright, good. Sit the rest of this drill out. But you're due back up for the next one," Luka said, patting her on the shoulder before skating off to watch the others practice.

Joey turned to leave the ice, catching Colton's gaze

before she could. He gave her a thumbs-up. She dramatically rolled her eyes at him.

Still, she had to admit she felt a little better knowing that Colton and Luka were looking out for her. Maybe the rest of the season wouldn't be so bad, after all.

25

The next day in school, Mr. Hoover stood in front of the science class, leaning against his desk. "Your genetics projects are due first thing Monday morning, and then we'll be moving on to a new exciting unit. But we'll talk about that when the time comes. For now, I want you to meet with your partners so you can really start finalizing your work together."

Which meant, of course, that Joey was going to have to work with Layla.

Colton didn't even hesitate to leave his desk so Layla could swap with him. Layla sat down, opened her notebook, and started to work quietly. Joey wasn't sure if she should say something. What *should* she say? Hi? What do you need me to do for this project? How's the weather?

But then Layla handed Joey a sheet of paper. "Fill this out" was all she said, before leaning back in her seat and away from Joey.

"Okay," Joey said. It was the same sheet of paper Layla had made at the start of the project, with Joey and her brothers' names written down the side in four rows, and her moms' up at the top in two columns. Layla had crossed out the spot for the donor.

Which was for the best, since they never even found out his name. "Mama deactivated the 23andMe account," Joey suddenly admitted.

Layla glanced sidelong at her. "Oh?"

"She said it wasn't safe," Joey said. "She, uh, said she'd help me find out options, if I really wanted. But that we went about it all wrong."

Layla got quiet again before saying, "Oh."

"I know it makes you and your mom happy, but it's different." Joey hesitated. "My family is different."

"I never said your family wasn't, but that never mattered to me, you know that," Layla said quickly.

"And I told you that you should have told your moms to begin with. I printed out all those resources for you."

"No, I know that, Layla. I'm just trying to say, sometimes the genealogy stuff makes me feel weird, when you talk about it."

Layla looked down at the papers in front of them. "We really should get this project done."

Joey sighed but started filling out the chart. She wrote down all of the things that Colton and Thomas had in common with Mama: Thomas and Mama's donkey laugh, all of their hair and eyes and skin color. Joey even wrote down how both Mama and Colton hated when anyone else was fighting. They liked to make everything right again. Mama's dad, their grandpa, was tall like the boys were, and Thomas, like Mama, was good at computers.

"Is the genealogy stuff why you didn't want to be my friend?" Layla suddenly asked, as she watched Joey's pen move against the paper. "Because, I'm sorry. I didn't know."

"No, that's not it," Joey said, swallowing hard. "I already told you why."

"I wish you didn't leave Jackson's that night," Layla said.

"I had to," Joey said, trying to focus on the project.

"You didn't," Layla said. "And I'm kind of sick and tired of you messing with me."

"I'm not messing with . . ." Joey started, but then stopped. "I'm trying to just make things easier for you. I'm trying not to hurt you, like I always do."

Layla scoffed. "You doing *this* hurts me and if you were gonna just decide to push me away again you never should have asked me for help in the first place."

Joey leaned forward and whispered, "I kissed you." She glanced around the room to make sure no one was listening. "Like, legit kissed you."

Layla nodded. "Yes."

"Yeah. So . . ." Joey didn't really know what she was supposed to say next. "So, I'm sorry, or whatever, I guess."

"You guess you're sorry?" Layla asked.

"I don't know what you want me to say. I don't really know what I'm supposed to do," Joey admitted.

"Are you sorry you kissed me?" Layla asked.

Joey shook her head. "Well, no. I mean, maybe? I don't . . ."

"If you asked me, I would have said yes," Layla said.

Which stunned Joey still. "What?"

"You keep deciding things about us without talking to me. You're saying you decided to stop being my friend the first time because you thought you'd hurt me. And then you decided to stop again now because you kissed me. *I'm* not afraid, you're the one who's afraid," Layla said.

"You two chatting or working over there?" Mr. Hoover called.

"Working," Layla and Joey both said at the same time.

"Wait," Joey said, replaying the conversation in her head. "If I had asked . . . if I could kiss you . . . you'd have said yes? You want to . . ."

Layla's cheeks were pink as she fiddled with the pen in her hand. "Yeah. I mean, I did. But I can't keep doing this thing where you want to be my friend and then don't want to be my friend. You're driving me crazy, Joey."

Despite everything else Layla was saying, Joey couldn't help the smile suddenly on her face. She thought she might even start laughing.

"Stop smiling!" Layla said, though she started smiling, too. "I'm mad at you!"

"I'm sorry, Layla," Joey said. "I'm sorry for a whole bunch of things lately, but I really am trying to be better."

Layla let out a big exhale. "Yeah, yeah. I know. I talk to Colton all the time. I *might* always make him tell me all about you."

Joey couldn't help herself. "You do?"

Layla tapped the paper in front of Joey. "I do. Now can you please just finish this chart so we can actually get an A on this project? No offense, but I am one hundred percent *done* with genetics."

"Honestly?" Joey said. "Me, too."

They fell quiet again, this time comfortably, as Layla watched Joey fill out the chart. She filled out Mama's rows with Thomas and Colton first, then moved to Mom and Benny. She moved to Thomas and Mom, to Colton and Mom, to Benny and Mama. Joey did everyone else first, before moving to her own row. She filled it out the best she could, as honestly as she could. No one shared her anger, but Mom was stubborn, Mom had a temper. There were things Joey shared with all of them, when she thought about it.

When she finished, she and Layla looked down at that chart. The result took Joey by surprise. "Should we change our hypothesis?" Layla asked.

Joey shook her head. "No. We should keep it just like this."

"I think you're right," Layla said, smiling.

"Maybe I can come over after school? We can write up the research paper part together?"

"Actually, I told Colton he and me can hang after school today. I thought about what you said. He's my best friend, too, and I hate thinking he feels left out. Is that okay?" Layla asked.

Joey nodded. "That's definitely okay."

"For now, I can take this home and have my mom get a big poster board or something? You can get photos of your family, and come over this weekend?" Layla said.

But as Joey looked down at that chart, she asked,

"Actually, can I take it home? And then maybe you can come over my place, instead, sometime this week."

Joey wanted to be done with this project. She wanted to finish it and put it behind her.

There was just something she knew she needed to do first.

26

Joey sat on the staircase, listening to the sounds of the movie her moms were watching together in the living room. She couldn't see them from where she was sitting, separated by the wall, but she knew what they'd look like, anyway. Mom was probably draped along the couch, Mama lying on top of her between her legs. They were mushy like that, especially when it was just the two of them.

Joey wanted that someday.

The paper she and Layla had been working on was folded in her hands. She was waiting for the right moment to interrupt them. Actually, she had been waiting for that moment all night.

She stood, walked down the rest of the stairs, and turned the corner to find her moms in the exact position she had expected. Mama had her hands covering her eyes, with only a little space to peek through. The music on the TV grew intense, and then there was a loud bang that had Mama jumping with a little shriek and Mom using her own hand to help cover Mama's face.

Mama was a bit of a scaredy-cat.

"Moms?" Joey said, and both of them jumped, startled, before realizing it was just her. Joey tried not to laugh.

Mom paused the TV. "Your timing could be better, Little Growl. Everything okay?"

"I, um, wanted to show you something," Joey said, running her fingers over the edges of the paper in her hands.

"Oh yeah? Make room, Mama," Mom said, pushing Mama up and off her as she turned to a more sitting position. Mama laughed as she shifted over a bit on the couch, patting the now-empty space between them.

Joey sat down, a mom on either side of her. Mama, the cuddler, wrapped an arm around her, pulling her even closer. Mama kissed Joey on the forehead, her hair tickling Joey's cheek, and Joey felt ready to talk to them now. "I wanted to show you guys something. From my and Layla's science project. The one on genetics."

"Genetics," Mom said, rolling her eyes. "Of *course* that's what this is about."

The way she said it made Joey stiffen, her hands fisting and crumpling the paper she was holding. "Forget it," she said, squirming out of Mama's arms to climb off the couch. "Never mind."

"Wait, wait, wait," Mom said, reaching for Joey and pulling her back in. "I'm sorry. I didn't mean to . . . I'm sorry, come here."

Joey let Mom drag her into her lap, arms wrapping tightly around her. Mama leaned in even closer, making Joey feel as though she was in a mom-sandwich again. She kept scowling, though, feeling the blush in her cheeks. She *had* been ready to talk about it, but now she was kind of embarrassed.

"Hey, seriously, Little Growl," Mom said. "I'm sorry. Talk to us."

"Why do you call me that?" Joey asked. "It makes me sound . . ."

Mom paused for a moment, and Joey wondered if

she said something again to hurt her. "I never meant it like how the boys called you Bruiser. It's just, you were always our little, you know. You'd watch those animal shows with Mama and growl, and you were always so . . . Okay, yeah. You scowled so much even when you were little, I just . . . started. I can stop? Do you want me to stop?"

Joey shrugged. "I don't know. I used to like it? But lately, everything's been . . . I was worried, and . . ." She didn't know how to have this conversation. They were getting off track as it was, and she almost wished she hadn't interrupted their movie in the first place.

Mama seemed to notice, running a soothing palm up and down Joey's arm. "What did you want to show us?"

Joey bit the inside of her cheek and unfolded the now-wrinkled paper in her hands. "We had to do a study on nature versus nurture. It was Layla's idea, but we're doing our project on our family. But our hypothesis ended up being wrong."

"It's okay to get it wrong," Mama said. "That's how scientists learn, right? They don't know everything going in."

Joey nodded. "I know. See, look. Our hypothesis

was basically that nature is more important than nurture. That genetics is what makes us who we are. Layla wrote down all of our names, and I was supposed to list the things we had in common. All of the traits that make us who we all are and stuff."

Joey didn't want to look Mom in the face. Not yet. She glanced over at Mama, though, who nodded, encouraging Joey to continue.

"I thought Colton, Thomas, and me would have the most in common with Mama. And that Benny would have the most in common with Mom," Joey said. "But . . ."

Mom reached to take the paper from Joey. She didn't say anything, just looked at it. It was Mama who finished Joey's sentence: "The longest list is you and Mom."

It was true. Joey and Mom were both stubborn. They both easily lost their tempers. They both liked ketchup on their scrambled eggs, and they both had a hard time opening up in therapy. They both were afraid of hurting the people they loved. They both hated wearing dresses. The list went on and on.

Mom was quiet, and Joey felt a little sweaty. "Mama

and Benny have a lot in common, too. Well, we all do, I guess."

Mom took a deep wobbly breath, quietly laughing as she wiped at her cheeks. She held Joey even closer. "Thank you," she whispered.

There was a lot Joey still didn't know. A lot of hypotheses still unanswered, a lot of things she was still worried about. She still wasn't super thrilled about having to talk to Dr. Collins. Part of her was still afraid she would do something that could push her moms, her brothers, away. Benny was still staying mostly with his dad, Thomas was still worried she'd be mean to him, Joey was still scared she could hurt Layla. The stitches on Mama's head would be removed, the cut would heal and fade, but Joey knew she would see that look on Mama's face after she hit the ground for a long, long time.

There was still a part of Joey that wondered about the donor.

"I love you," Mom said.

"We both do," Mama added.

Joey smiled. She didn't have all the answers yet, but she had a new hypothesis, with her moms, and a new plan. They would try new things and hopefully find the answers. They would try and maybe they would fail, but just like any good scientists they would try again. They would *keep* trying.

And maybe Joey would always have that tight feeling in her chest. Maybe she would always have that need to start screaming.

But now that her moms were listening, now that they were trying to understand, Joey could close her eyes, enjoy the feeling of their arms wrapped around her, and feel hopeful.

ACKNOWLEDGMENTS

I wrote the first draft of this book very early on in the pandemic, around April 2020, so I'd like to thank everything that got me through those early days of quarantine: Rook Coffee (to which I almost dedicated this entire book); *The Circle* on Netflix; restaurants that offered takeout; the classic pizza and jalapeño dip from Old Glory; disco fries from Yellow Rose; and *every. Single. Thing* at Neelam Exotic Indian Cuisine. The homemade bagels my wife learned to make (notice most of these are food); the cider-making kit my brother bought me for my birthday; my Androgynous Fox sweatpants; my FLAVNT sweatpants; all my pairs of sweatpants; the Nintendo Switch we had to stalk Target to grab the minute it finally was in stock; Laura Dern, Teri Polo, and the ability to stream movies starring pretty women whose faces could distract me from anything. And to the friends who happy-hour-Zoomed with us, cheers.

To my agent, Jim McCarthy: thank you, again and always, for your patience with me and my ever-growing list of projects that I email you about constantly. I hope you didn't think the pandemic would slow me down when it did quite literally the opposite. You're a champ. Seriously.

To my editor, Krestyna Lypen: I've never had to think twice about trusting my work in your hands, and I'm realizing just how very lucky I am to be able to say that.

Everyone at Algonquin: thank you again, and again, and again, for always making me feel safe with you all, as an author and human and little anxious toad.

Liz, you are my Theo, my wuffenloaf, and now I can add *wife* to that list, too.

Mom and Dad and Matthew, I wrote in this book that biology does not make a family, but I'm thankful in our case that it also did.

And, most importantly, to every single middle schooler who has reached out to me to tell me your story: I still hear and see you, and I always will.